I Am Arthur Bright

I Am Arthur Bright
An Alzheimer's Story

Julian Lovelock

The Critical Forum

First published in 2024 by The Critical Forum
books@thecriticalforum.co.uk

Copyright © 2024 Julian Lovelock

ISBN 978-0-9550433-1-4

All rights reserved. No part of this edition may be reproduced, stored electronically or in any retrieval system, or transmitted in any form or by any means, electronic, mechanical, photocopying, recording, or otherwise, without prior written permission from the publisher.

FOR DAVID AND ANTHEA

With love and thanks

I

Alice in Wonderland

Arthur opens the book clumsily, runs his fingers over the photographs, some half-remembered, some not at all, and tries to make sense of ~~the~~ words that surround them. He looks up and watches the blue tits pecking busily at the rusting feeder outside. The wisteria is in purple bloom and the musky scent drifts through the open window. It reminds of somewhere familiar he cannot quite place. Books have been at the centre of Arthur's life – he has read them avidly, written and collected them, bought and sold – but they have become another part of the past that is slipping inexorably away. Now the book he holds is the only one left to him and the only one that matters. And even that confuses him. A yellow brimstone butterfly perches delicately on the window frame, looking in.

Arthur does not know how the confusion started. Perhaps it did start with the words, an insidiously creeping dysphasia. Once upon a time they had leapt at his command, but one by one they had disappeared in a cruel game of hide-and-seek and only the well-thumbed thesaurus could help him find them. He had started to begin sentences but lost where they were going. When he wrote, he had to stop and think back to pick up the thread; when he spoke, the meaning was too often left hanging in the air. Once upon a time… But then, 'He's not with it these days, it's such a dreadful shame,' people had whispered and had looked at each other knowingly, and soon they had hurriedly crossed the street to avoid his circular conversations. Or perhaps it had started before that, when he had forgotten which of the kitchen cupboards held what and kept putting things back in the wrong place. 'You must be losing your memory, Arthur,' Mary had said, laughingly, as she took the salt and pepper from the fridge, and he had laughed too. Until, that is, she had known it was not a joke at all and wept silently. Not long ago they had celebrated their golden wedding anniversary – fifty years, although it had not usually felt that long – but they were still in their mid-seventies, not old enough for things to go so disastrously wrong.

And this is where Arthur has washed up, another piece of life's splintered wreckage: the Marsh View Care Home. He has been here for five weeks now. It is what Mary had not wanted – she had promised faithfully she would never put him in a home – and he had not wanted it either. He sits not altogether upright in the red, easy-clean vinyl chair, not quite knowing where he is: a diminished figure, with thinning grey hair and uneven patches of stubble the razor has left behind. Once he was particular about his dress, but his clothes have somehow outgrown him. His baggy maroon sweater hangs limply over his hands and his carpet-slippered feet are swamped by his grey-flannel trousers. A line of poetry learned long ago at Burgoyne floats to the surface, though he cannot quite place it: 'I grow old ... I grow old ... I shall wear the bottom of my trousers rolled.' And wasn't there something about eating peaches and mermaids singing?

Arthur looks down at the book. His photograph is on the glossy hardback cover, a young man in suntanned health on a sandy beach with Mary and the children (Florence and Maria, though for the moment he does not remember their names, or which is which, or when he last saw them). It was taken many years ago, when there were buckets and spades, sandcastles with flags, ice creams with chocolate flakes, and the sky was always blue. ***I AM ARTHUR***

BRIGHT, the title announces boldly, a defiant statement of identity, and, in smaller letters, **And This Is My Story**. Prompted by the Matron at Marsh View, Flo and Maria had spent an afternoon at Rose Bank combing the treasure-trove of fading papers and family albums, discovering things about their parents they had never known (although there were other things they did not discover which would, with luck, remain secret until the end of time). Afterwards, Maria had scanned their favourite photographs and composed the simple text to go with them, and Clearprint had done the rest. Flo and Maria were delighted with the slim volume that arrived, neatly packaged, in the post, but they are understandably biased. In truth, it manages only to reduce an unremarkable life into a few shiny pages – a collection of facts and highlights that is not really Arthur's story at all; and because he has not told the story himself, it is not even lifted by the rosy glow of nostalgia. But the book is important to Arthur because it helps him cling for a little longer to years gone by and to that extent it is a success. He keeps it hidden in the small antique desk he was allowed to bring with him and is puzzled each time he finds it. He has never seen it before.

There is a tap at the door. 'Come in.' Arthur's once magisterial voice has faded along with his memory.

'Hello, Arthur. It's Alice. And how are you this sunny afternoon? I'm just bringing your tea.' Outwardly, Alice is unfailingly sunny. She puts his tea on the yellow Formica table beside him – a gold-rimmed cup and saucer. She knows Arthur does not like mugs and she tries to do things properly for him. She had bought the cup and saucer herself in the local *Oxfam* shop. There is a slightly curled sandwich and a small slice of Victoria sponge. Once Arthur had enjoyed his food – even all those years of school food – but his sense of taste is no longer what it was and this is pale and insipid.

'Alice … in wonderland?' says Arthur.

Alice smiles. She is young – probably in her early twenties – fair-haired, grey-eyed, in a crisply ironed sky-blue uniform. That is what Arthur always says. 'Yes, Arthur, that's right. Alice in wonderland.' She likes Arthur. He is a gentleman and polite, even on his down days. She thinks about the Mad Hatter's tea party, but in a kindly way. 'Is that your special book, Arthur?'

Arthur looks enquiringly at the book and at the lined, liver-spotted hands that hold it, unsure where it has come from. 'I suppose it is. Would you ... like to see?'

Alice kneels beside him and turns to the first page: she might have been one of his pupils. It has become a ritual of which she never tires. For Arthur it is always new. 'I am Arthur Bright,' reads Alice. 'I was born on 16 October 1944 in Hartbourne, a village near Grantham in Lincolnshire where I lived with my mother and her parents.' A sepia photograph shows a coyly posed couple in Edwardian dress. In the background are a pier (penny for the frilly-knickered peep show) and the shimmering, sail-spotted sea. 'These are Grandpa and Grandma on their honeymoon.' The young Grandpa is tall, with a mop of dark, curly hair and strong, skilled hands – a cabinet maker, one of the best in the area, always in demand; the young Grandma is small, fair-haired, alert – a nurse in Grantham's hospital until their daughter was born. 'They look lovely, Arthur,' says Alice, 'and they're so full of life, aren't they? Are they your grandpa and grandma?'

Arthur screws up his eyes and looks more closely at the photograph. A smile of half-recognition creeps across his face. 'Yes ... I think they are,' he says slowly.

'Do you remember them, your grandpa and grandma?'

'Oh yes. We lived with them ... my mother and I ... and they looked after me a lot. There was a big table in the kitchen, and the smell ... freshly baked bread. And scones and ... jam. In winter there was a roaring ... fire in the living room and we ... toasted ... crumpets. Later there was a television. Only black-and-white ... a very small ... screen in ...' He pauses, as he often does, searching for the words. 'In a large ... walnut ... cabinet. We thought it was ... magic. *Bill and Ben, the Flowerpot Men ... Sooty and ...*' It is strange how the earliest memories are the ones that last the longest.

'What were their names?' asks Alice.

Arthur thinks for a bit, wrinkles his already furrowed brow. 'Grandpa and Grandma,' he says at last. 'They were Grandpa and Grandma.' He studies the picture again. 'Sometimes they took me ... on the train to the seaside ... at Skeggy. I suppose you've never ... been on a steam train?'

'No, but I've seen them at the pictures. In *Strangers on a Train* and *Murder on the Orient Express*.'

Arthur does not remember the strangers or the Orient Express. Instead, he is thinking back to his childhood and seeing his own moving pictures of those special days not yet quite forgotten. Striped deckchairs. Catching crabs in the slipping-over rock pools. Collecting shells that sounded of the sea: listen, you can hear the waves and the mermaids singing. Skimming stones. Building barricades and battling against the tide. Sometimes Punch and Judy – the sausages and the crocodile. 'And Grandpa went to sleep and the wind blew his ... newspaper ... and I ran after it ... all the way ... into the water. And Grandma had made a picnic, with sausage rolls and homemade ... And later we'd walk back ... to the station ... go home ... tea.'

Arthur stops, struggling to focus his inner projector, which is clattering to a halt. He takes a sip of his weak and lukewarm tea. He looks up at Alice and thinks he might have seen her somewhere before. 'Are you ... Alice?' he asks.

Alice smiles at him warmly. 'Yes, Arthur. Alice in wonderland'. He has asked the question a hundred times or more, but there is no hint of irritation in her voice. She is just pleased that today is one of his good days and he is remembering. When his mind wanders, she helps him turn the page. Here there is a wedding photograph of his parents: the slim bride in a long and lacy dress, with a posy of spring flowers, radiating happiness ('Arthur, you look so like your mother'); the groom, with handsome, clear-cut features, standing tall in his army uniform, his sergeant's stripes clearly visible. The photograph had once stood in an always polished silver frame on the sideboard at Hartbourne. 'These are Iris and … Lionel, my mother … and father,' reads Arthur haltingly. 'They met at a dance before the … war and married in September 1943 when my father was on … leave. He was killed a year later on the … Normandy beaches. He was awarded a … Distinguished Conduct Medal for gallantry in action … against the enemy.' Iris had kept the medal safely in her jewellery box and sometimes she had taken it out, felt the ribbon, cradled the ice-cold metal in her longing hands, and thought bitterly of the courage and the waste, and how both their futures had been left bleeding on the sea-washed sands.

'You must be so proud of him, Arthur,' says Alice.

Arthur says nothing. He had never known his father and his mother had scarcely spoken of him. She had poured her love into Arthur and he into her, but she had never stopped being sad. And there came a time when it dawned on him he had never known his father's parents either. What was all that about? Did they even know he existed? Something told him he should not ask. He can just about recall how Grandpa and Grandma had looked after him when his mother took a part-time job to supplement her war widows' pension, and how, when he turned five, he had gone to the village school. He had been shy at first, not used to lots of other children, but he had loved books and loved learning to read, and soon he was running and shouting with the rest in the rough-and-tumble, tag-playing playground. Arthur Bright, one of the gang.

There is another photograph: eleven well-scrubbed children and their teacher, smartly arranged in front of the red-brick school building with its high windows. 'This is me at Hartbourne School,' reads Alice. 'I am second from the left at the front.' Young Arthur is taller than the others, a skinny lad with nondescript hair and a nervous, self-conscious smile. 'Do you remember any of their names, Arthur?' she asks.

Arthur looks curiously at the photograph. After a time he points to a lad with a fringe, a sprinkling of freckles and a cheeky grin. 'That's Norman. ... He was my best friend.' Norman had lived with his parents and an older sister in a cottage on the edge of the village. In the school holidays he and Arthur had often played together and there had been sleepovers, usually at Norman's cottage, before sleepovers were fashionable. Arthur had always felt comfortable at the cottage and only much later did he realise that Norman's parents were giving his mother and his grandparents a needed break. Then Arthur points to a plump, blond-haired girl. 'And that's ... Sarah. She lived next door to us.' He pauses. 'I liked Sarah. She was a bit older. ... We used to go for walks ... in the fields and woods ... nothing happened.' After a while, he points to the prim, grey-haired teacher. 'That's Mrs Jones. She was very strict ... very kind.' But Arthur is still thinking of Sarah.

'I don't know how you remember them all.' Time and again Alice is surprised how Arthur can remember names from seventy years ago, but nothing from yesterday or even today.

'I must go to see ... my mother,' says Arthur. 'I need to see her.'

'I think she's gone out today, Arthur.' Alice lays her hand on his arm. 'Perhaps tomorrow, eh?' She has learned that a small untruth is better than a truth he cannot grasp. She points again at the photograph, trying to hold his attention.

'I don't think ... she's out,' says Arthur. 'Have you ever been ... on a steam train?'

'No, I haven't. They don't have steam trains anymore. But I've seen them at the pictures.'

'Grandpa and Grandma used to take me ... to the seaside ... on a train as a treat,' says Arthur. He begins to look worried and struggles to get up. 'I must go to … see my mother.'

'She won't be home yet,' says Alice. 'I'd go a bit later, Arthur, if I were you.'

In the distance the doorbell rings. The trickle of apprehensive visitors to Marsh View means it often rings. 'Is that the bell?' asks Arthur. His life as a schoolmaster had been ruled by a timetable of bells. 'I mustn't be … late for lessons.'

Alice is not sure if he is joking. 'No, Arthur. It's just someone at the door.' Saved by the bell,' she thinks, but not unpleasantly.

'For me?'

'I don't think so, but I'd better find out. I'll be back in a jiffy – and don't forget your tea.'

'Do you have to go?'

'I'm afraid so, Arthur. Be good, won't you.'

Arthur smiles weakly. 'I'll try.' There is a distant twinkle in his eyes. 'I'm going to see … my mother later.'

Left alone, Arthur takes another sip of tea. It is barely warm and he pulls a disgusted face. He eats the curled sandwich and the cake, dropping crumbs into his lap. A spot of thin, seedless jam dribbles onto his sweater, adding a new stickiness to the growing collection of stains. He wonders when that nice Alice will come to see him. It's some time since she's been. He picks up the book again and looks inquiringly at the cover. ***I AM ARTHUR BRIGHT … And This Is My Story.***

*

Very slowly time passes, although day and night mean less and less to Arthur. When his muddle began, Mary had bought one of those clocks with a bold display which showed the day of the week and whether it was morning or afternoon, but Arthur had got into the habit of switching it off at the wall ('Just to be safe') and its blank screen only mirrored his confusion. Every morning one of the carers looks into his room and, if he is awake, brings his breakfast – the milky tea, cereal (cornflakes, always cornflakes) and toast, already cold. Later they will change his pad, help him wash and dress, and sit him in his chair. Arthur has been the most placid of men, but occasionally and without warning he rages at the indignity of it all. 'Do not go gentle into that good night,' he mutters to himself. Every evening they help him to his bed. But there are days when he sleeps and nights when he wakes and presses his call-button: he is worried he has missed his lunch. Or sometimes, in the dark hours, he manages to find the way out of his room and is walking unsteadily in his too big, checked pyjamas along the meandering and dimly lit corridor.

'Where are you off to, Arthur?' asks Alice. The mat outside his room has triggered an alarm.

Arthur looks at her – a face he recognises. 'You're Alice ... aren't you?'

'Yes, Arthur. Alice in wonderland.'

Arthur is puzzled. He is not sure where he is off to or where he is. 'I'm afraid I get in a bit of a ... muddle sometimes. I'm not sure where I am. ... Have I had my ... lunch yet?'

'It's the middle of the night, Arthur, you sausage.' Alice takes his arm; her touch is warm and comforting. 'Come on, let's get you back to bed.'

'Is my mother ... all right?'

'She's fine. Arthur. Let's think about that in the morning.'

'Isn't it morning? Oh dear ... I'm sorry to be such a ... nuisance.'

'You're not a nuisance, Arthur. We're just having a little walk.'

'It's Alice, isn't it,' says Arthur as she checks his pad and helps him into bed.'

'That's right, Arthur,' she says, squeezing his hand. 'Alice in wonderland. I'll see you tomorrow.'

In the rosy glow from the nightlight Arthur wonders where he is and what is happening to him. Is he back at Sparrowhawk, in the dormitory, hoping his mother is all right? Is it Sparrowhawk's matron who has just been to see him? The sun is beginning to creep through the thin curtains when at last he drifts off to sleep. He is still asleep when Alice peeps round the door and she is careful not to disturb him. He does not hear the mocking cry of the seagulls which have drifted inland. Who knows where he is in his dreams?

*

Another indistinguishable day. A fly buzzes at the window, trying frantically to escape. Arthur is holding his book and looking at a picture of his mother, taken in 1953. She is smiling at the camera, but she looks pallid and unwell, and the smile does little to hide her unhappiness. 'My mother fell ill in 1953,' reads Alice. 'She passed away in the summer of 1954.' None of the pain of the last year of her life is mentioned. The death certificate stated 'complications arising from pneumonia': her lungs had always been weak, but the truth was a shattered heart that could not be put back together. She had never recovered from Lionel's death and, without the will to live without him, not even her love for Arthur could save her. Nor, of course, is there any reference to Arthur's misery in that dreadful year, when his grandparents had not told him how ill his mother was. Instead, they told him she would soon be better and he was not to worry. But Arthur was old enough to know they might be lying, and old enough to go along with the lie for his mother's sake. 'Oh, Arthur', says Alice, 'how horrible for you. I'm so sorry.'

Even now, Arthur can recall how the Christmas of 1953 was a glittering sham and how the tinselled tree, the gaudy homemade paper chains, and the mountain of gaily wrapped presents had done nothing to raise his spirits. In later years he would realise guiltily that his mother had simply wanted to make it a special time for them both. Deep down she had accepted it would be their last Christmas together and his misery had spoiled it for her. When, in the February frosts, her condition took another turn for the worse, it was decided he should be spared her agony and the rasping cough that echoed through the house, and should go away to school. Letters were written, prospectuses studied, and visits made. Arthur was never consulted.

So that April, after a flurry of shopping for uniform, sewing of nametapes, checking of clothes lists and the careful packing of an enormous trunk, Grandpa's car was loaded for the thirty-mile drive to Sparrowhawk Hall. Grandma sat in the front, trying to make cheerful conversation, while Arthur and his mother sat closely together in the back: she had been determined to make the journey with him. Sparrowhawk Hall stood on a hill on a bend in the road, screened by tall and gloomy conifers. It was, thought Arthur, like a story-book school, a Victorian pile of grey stone, with a short flight of steps leading up to the imposing oak front-door (forbidden to pupils, except at the beginning and end of term), and a castellated gothic tower perched incongruously at each extremity.

Grandpa parked the car on the sweeping gravel drive. No sooner had he opened the boot than a smartly dressed porter lifted out Arthur's trunk and wooden tuckbox and spirited them away. An elegant, heavily made-up lady approached and bent down to the rear window. Arthur's mother wound it down. 'Welcome to Sparrowhawk Hall, Mrs Bright. It's so good to see you again.' The lady turned her attention to Arthur. 'And this handsome young man must be Arthur. I'm Mrs Cholmondeley-Robinson – the headmaster's wife. Aren't you going to get out, Arthur, and say hello?'

'Go on, Arthur,' whispered his mother, her voice trembling.

Nervously, Arthur climbed out. Mrs Cholmondeley-Robinson held out her hand. 'Good afternoon, Arthur,' she gushed. 'I'm sure we're going to be the very best of friends.'

Arthur knew he was expected to shake hands. 'Good afternoon,' he said politely. He was not going to risk saying her name and her cold, limp fingers gave him the creeps, so he was not sure about their being best friends either.

'Now, kiss your mother goodbye', said Mrs Cholmondeley-Robinson briskly, 'and we'll go to find your dormitory.'

The parting was over in moments – Mrs Cholmondeley-Robinson was like a skilful dentist extracting a tooth – though for Arthur the hurt would never wholly go away. Clutching Mrs Cholmondeley-Robinson's fishy fingers with one hand and his brown leather overnight case with the other, he walked determinedly up the steps. He was not going to turn round and show his mother he was crying, which was just as well, since both she and Grandma were sobbing too. 'He'll be fine, Iris, don't you worry, and it'll be half-term before you know it,' said Grandpa as he started the car.

That night, in the dormitory (black, steel-framed beds; grey, army-surplus blankets; a row of cracked washbasins; bare wooden floor), Arthur listened to the breathing of his companions. Some had been at Sparrowhawk for a year or more and ignored the new boys, except to boss them about. There were whispers, too quiet to make out, and a torch flashed briefly. From a far corner of the room came muffled, homesick tears, but Arthur was resigned to what was happening to him and soon lapsed into a troubled sleep.

In Arthur's book, there is a photograph of him looking sheepish in a bright-red blazer and grey corduroy shorts: 'My First Day at Sparrowhawk Hall'.

*

On Sunday, supervised by the grumpy duty master – Arthur had not yet found out his name – he wrote his first letter home. The sort of things he was expected to say were written on the blackboard. Anything that suggested unhappiness or reflected badly on Sparrowhawk Hall was forbidden and the letter would have to be written again.

Dear Mummy

I like it at Sparowhawk Hall and I have made some new frends. I like the food and the lessons and yesterday we played criket and I scored five runs. I'm reeding a book from the libry called biggles. The teachers are very nice.

We're not aloud to talk after lights out or we get the cane. Ouch. This afternoon we are going for a walk in the rain and my new welington boots.

I hope you are feeling better. I look forwood to seeing you soon.

Yours Sincerly, Bright

Arthur handed the letter to the master who cast a cursory eye over it. 'Not very bright at spelling, are we Bright? And I didn't know the library was called Biggles. But I suppose it'll do.' Arthur did not think much of the master's jokes and noticed the biscuit crumbs nestling in his untended, bristly moustache, but with some relief he folded the letter into the self-addressed envelope his mother had given him and left it in the pile with the others. Then he walked back disconsolately to his desk and to Biggles, rolling his eyes as he went.

Iris was not quite sure what to make of the letter when it arrived and sensed that Arthur was already slipping away from her. She hated the idea of him being caned: there was nothing about that in the prospectus, which promised a happy and caring place. Grandpa said Arthur would have been laughed at if he'd sent love and kisses, and hoped he'd soon be taught to spell properly. Nearly seventy years later, Flo and Maria would find the letter, still in its envelope, and laughed aloud. 'Poor Dad!' It had to go into Arthur's book.

*

Arthur gradually made friends at Sparrowhawk – and, as luck would have it, their names were squashed together with his when the class register was read each morning: 'Barnes, Belcher, Bingham, Bowler, Bowring, Bright …'

'All present, Sir!'

The boys were very different. Barnes, a new boy like Arthur, was a melancholy lad who would often retreat into his own private world; Belcher was large and loud, with ginger hair, and was the butt of jokes that never seemed to faze him; Bingham – 'Specs' on account of his horn-rimmed spectacles – was a swat and the masters' favourite; Bowler, who was constantly on the move, was already good at sport and a natural leader; Bowring (the Honourable Bowring) was a chaotic character, forever losing things and forever late. In break-times and after lessons the six of them could usually be found together, playing raucous games, making camps in the wooded grounds and planning impossible adventures.

It was these friends who helped Arthur largely to forget about home, but twice a week, when the post was handed out at breakfast, he would recognise the distinctive cream envelope. There was never much news – just what Grandpa and Grandma had been up to, some tittle-tattle about the neighbours, and occasional tales of goings-on at the village school which amused him. He wondered what mischief Norman had been getting up to. For a moment he would wish he was back with his mother, helping to look after her, and he noticed how frail her once strong handwriting had become. But she said she was feeling better and was looking forward to seeing him, and when the bell sounded for lessons he was again swallowed up in Sparrowhawk's relentless routine.

*

Two days before half-term. Arthur woke up sensing something was wrong. He did not know what or why but, try as he might, he could not rid it from his mind. After lunch he walked nervously down the polished passageway which led to Mr Cholmondeley-Robinson's study. The walls were hung with dark portraits of previous Sparrowhawk headmasters. Only one let slip the trace of a smile, and that was ironic. Arthur had never been here before – it was the place you were sent when you were in trouble – but this was important. He knocked bravely on the brass-handled door.

'In!' The response was a harsh bird-call.

Cautiously Arthur opened the door and went in. He looked down at his feet. The carpet was a dull maroon, a little threadbare, heavily patterned. There was a stone fireplace, its hearth enclosed by a brass fender with a green leather seat. Baskets of logs stood on either side, but there was nothing to show the fire had ever been lit. In the middle of the room was a low oak coffee table and two stick-back Windsor chairs. On the marble mantelpiece were polished silver cups for 'Boxing', 'Shooting', 'Endeavour', 'Leadership', and the like, which were awarded each term and then, engraved at the recipient's expense, returned immediately to their appointed place; above them was a faded print of bathers on a riverbank. To Arthur's left hung a signed light-blue college oar with a group of fading black-and-white photographs of a rowing eight – only the most observant would have noticed that Cholmondeley-Robinson's signature did not appear on the oar, nor did he feature in the photographs: he had bought them as a job-lot at a local auction many years before. To Arthur's right, on a mahogany side-table, an ornate silver salver held a decanter of whisky, a single lead-crystal glass and a small jug of water. A chipped china umbrella stand sported a collection of evil-looking canes.

Mr Cholmondeley-Robinson looked up quizzically from his desk. He was like an ageing bird of prey: black, frayed gown; greying hair, brilliantined back; cruel, darting eyes; aquiline nose; long neck that tilted his head slightly forward; fingers that were hard and slender, like claws. 'Beaky' the boys called him, though never within his hearing. Arthur wondered if the school was named after him. 'Well, Bright, to what do I owe this, erm, pleasure?' asked Mr Cholmondeley-Robinson in his rasping, reedy voice. 'Not in any trouble, I hope?' He glanced hopefully at the canes.

'No, sir.'

'Well, Bright? Not many boys come to visit me if they're not in trouble.'

'Please, sir. I must go to see my mother, sir.'

Mr Cholmondeley-Robinson smiled. 'Must? There's no 'must' about it, Bright. It's half-term in a couple of days. You'll be seeing her then.'

He was trying to be kind, but Arthur thought not of kindness, nor even of birds, but of wolves. Oh Mr Cholmondeley-Robinson, what big teeth you have. ... All the better to bite me with, he thought. 'Yes, sir. But I think there's something wrong, sir.'

'And why do you think that, Bright?'

'I don't know, sir. I just do, sir.'

'If there's something wrong, your grandfather would have telephoned me.'

'Yes, sir. I suppose so, sir.'

'Perhaps you're just excited about going home?'

'Yes, sir. I mean, no, sir. There is something wrong, sir. I know it, sir.'

'You've had a good first-half, Bright, and I'll extol your virtues to your mother. She'll be proud of you.'

'Yes, sir. Thank you, sir.'

'Now, don't worry yourself, Bright. I'm sure everything's all right. Off you go now. We don't want to be late for cricket, do we?'

Arthur looked at Mr Cholmondeley-Robinson's teeth and his narrowed eyes, and at the canes which leered at him threateningly. He mumbled his insincere thanks and made his escape. He thought about running away, but there was nowhere to run and perhaps Beaky was right, Grandpa would have said if anything was amiss. And soon he'd be going home anyway.

The couple of days dragged by. It was the afternoon before half-term and, in the classroom, Mr Penfold attempted to amuse the over-excited members of form two. He was a fresh-faced man in his early thirties. His straight, sandy hair flopped over his forehead and he habitually swept it back with the palm of his hand. He was wearing the regulation summer uniform of a prep school master: navy blazer (with shiny elbows and chalked cuffs), light-grey flannel trousers, his own striped old school tie, and polished brown brogues. That night, as a treat, there would be end-of-term games and then secret midnight feasts when the boys would gorge themselves on tuck they had squirrelled away from their meagre rations. For now, though, there was one more pointless history lesson for them to endure. The early summer had been unusually hot and it would have been easier for the class to be taken outside onto the new-mown grass to tell sad stories of the death of kings and bloody battles long ago, even to act them out, but Mr Cholmondeley-Robinson disapproved of such levity. So, in the sweaty heat, the boys played a sort of 'bingo' with historical dates and hunted for the names of kings and queens, heroes and villains, hidden in a jumble of word-search letters. As the purple wisteria edging the window stirred in the breeze and the sun's rays dappled the not-so-old desks carved casually with names and imprecations, Arthur watched the mites of chalk dust which danced like an unseasonal and unhurried snowstorm. Outside, beautiful and transitory, peacock, red-admiral and cabbage-white butterflies settled on the buddleia, its blooms turning brown in the scorching heat; beyond, the cricket square was parched and worn, bearing the scars of another triumphant, joyless season. The faint hum of bees gathering pollen and the song of a lone blackbird only emphasised the heavy silence.

It was an aimless wasp, arriving by accident in the classroom, which provided the diversion for which the boys had been longing. Bowler was the first to raise the alarm: 'Wasp alert! Wasp alert!'

'Do be quiet, Bowler,' said Mr Penfold without conviction. He saw no reason to bring the class to heel until it had expended some of its pent-up excitement.

'Messerschmitt at five o'clock,' shouted Bowring. 'Dive! Dive!'

Barnes, who was genuinely frightened of wasps and most other things, saved face by diving under his desk, which promptly tipped over on top of him and cascaded its contents of books, papers and illicit sweets onto the ink-stained linoleum. Bingham ran to the door and stood guard, although with Mr Penfold supervising the class this was more an instinctive reaction and it was not clear who or what he was guarding against. Perhaps, as was his wont, he was trying to keep out of trouble. Arthur leapt onto his chair, swiping wildly with his exercise book at the wasp he could no longer see: 'Die, wasp! Die!'

'Rat-a-tat-a-tat-a-tat-a-tat!' This was Belcher, who had become the Lancaster tail-gunner, aiming his machine-gun ruler at nothing in particular.

'Pick up your desk, Barnes,' said Mr Penfold more sharply. 'Now.'

'Rat-a-tat-a-tat-a-tat!'

'Enough, Belcher. Enough …'

'Rat-a-tat-a-tat-a-tat!'

'Gotcha!' cried the Honourable Bowring, though not convincingly. The wasp continued on its increasingly desperate journey.

'Watch out!' hissed Bingham. But he was too late.

The door had opened silently and Mr Cholmondeley-Robinson materialised more than entered, like a magician's trick. He saw it all in a slow-motion that fixed itself into a tableau: boys frozen in mid-swipe or gun attack. His eyes lit instantly on Arthur, petrified with his exercise book held aloft, like a statue on a plinth.

'A little high-spirited, are we, Bright?' asked Mr Cholmondeley-

Robinson, in his reedy voice. 'Perhaps you'll come along with me?' He liked to pick on a boy and make a painful example of him. 'And a word later, perhaps, Mr Penfold? This behaviour really won't do.'

'Yes, sir. Sorry, sir,' muttered Arthur, his lip trembling. He was not so much worried for himself but for his mother if she saw the livid weals he knew the cane would leave behind. 'If you wish, Headmaster,' said Mr Penfold coldly.

For the moment after Mr Cholmondeley-Robinson departed with Arthur in tow, no-one moved or spoke. Beneath his still-upturned desk, Barnes whimpered. Amidst the chaos, the wasp had at last found the open window and freedom. Outside the bees still hummed, the blackbird sang and somewhere a lawnmower rattled. There were hushed exchanges: the boys knew what was likely to happen

'All right, boys, back to your desks,' sighed Mr Penfold, looking out across the cricket field. He too feared for Arthur and wondered why he stayed at Sparrowhawk, tacitly condoning such spite.

'Oh, sir,' said Belcher, 'do you think he'll get the whacks?' Belcher was an expert in being whacked, holding that year's record – nineteen – for beatings from Dr Graham. There was faint, nervous laughter.

'Bend over, Bright. Touch your toes. I'm going to give you six.' Belcher's speech was high and grating. With his right hand he waved an imaginary cane; with his left he gently rubbed his crotch. It was a meticulously observed impression, although barely understood. There were suppressed giggles. Mr Penfold turned away, hiding his own amusement. Gradually, almost half-heartedly, the chatter resumed, but in spite of Belcher's intervention the fun had gone. They were all wondering about Bright and waiting anxiously for his return.

*

Arthur followed Mr Cholmondeley-Robinson down the forbidding corridor. This time the portraits smirked at him as he passed. Outside the study, Mr Cholmondeley-Robinson turned to Arthur and beckoned him to a chair. 'Wait there, Bright.' He went into the study and closed the door. Arthur sensed the waiting and the fear were part of the punishment, but then he heard the clink of a cup and the low drone of conversation and was confused. He sat, head bowed, in his misery.

After what seemed an age, Mr Cholmondeley-Robinson came out of the study, not with his beady-eyed, angry look, but with a trace of his wolfish smile. 'Come along in, Bright, I've some people to see you.' As Arthur went nervously in, he saw, sitting on the Windsor chairs, Grandpa and Grandma. Grandma, weeping quietly, stood up slowly and put her arm around him. Arthur knew at once why he'd needed to see his mother.

'I'm afraid we have some bad news, Arthur,' said Grandpa.

'I told you I had to go,' Arthur half shouted at Mr Cholmondeley-Robinson, and buried his head against Grandma. 'I knew,' he grizzled, 'and you stopped me.'

As one by one Arthur's memories have disappeared, and even the earliest ones have worn at the edges, this memory has never left him. He sees it all quite clearly, as if he is watching a play and is also a member of the cast.

'I'll leave you for a bit,' said Mr Cholmondeley-Robinson, who was not very good with tears. 'I'm sure you'd like some time alone. Chin up, Bright.'

The journey home was passed largely in silence. There was nothing meaningful to be said. As they came to the village street, Arthur raised his reddened eyes. It was the same familiar place – the noisy school playground, the shop with its housewares stacked brashly outside, the telephone box and the bus stop nearby – but it all looked quite different. Everything had changed irrevocably.

*

Two weeks later, after the grim business of the funeral and the polite but comfortless condolences, Arthur returned to Sparrowhawk Hall. His friends did not know what to say, but 'Hard cheese, Bright,' ventured Bowler, and little by little his life returned to a sort of empty normal. He would spend four years at Sparrowhawk, where the Cholmondeley-Robinsons ran an increasingly creaky empire. His spelling improved, he evaded the wandering hands of the music master, and Mr Penfold's lessons inspired a lifelong love of history. Sparrowhawk was almost devoid of emotion and empathy, but it allowed Arthur to grieve silently. There were no intrusive questions, so no answers were needed. In fact, holidays with Grandpa and Grandma were more difficult for Arthur. There were too many reminders of his mother in every room, waiting to jump out at him, and too much well-meaning sympathy.

For many years afterwards, Arthur looked back on his time at Sparrowhawk Hall with a peculiar affection. In a way, it had been his salvation. Some of his best as well as his worst times were played out there and, after his mother's death, it became his family, albeit a dysfunctional one. He often wondered about the Cholmondeley-Robinsons. Would they have been different if they'd had their own children? They hadn't been wholly bad people; in a strange way they had probably cared, although less when they'd become tired of life at Sparrowhawk and the struggle to keep it afloat in changing times. He sometimes tried to imagine what their life had been like outside school, in their eyrie high up in the south tower. He had never seen a flicker of feeling pass between them. Mrs Cholmondeley-Robinson – secretary, factotum, accountant, matron – had been master as well as servant. Separate beds; perhaps separate rooms? Had they enjoyed the company of a circle of friends? It was unlikely: he had not seen any visitors. Sparrowhawk had moulded and consumed them. He felt pity as much as contempt.

On Arthur's last day at Sparrowhawk Hall, there was the final assembly with the rousing, lump-in-the-throat end-of-term hymn: 'Let thy father-hand be shielding / All who here shall meet no more...'. Then there were the ritual saying of goodbyes ('See you, Bright. Have a good hols!'), the swapping of addresses and telephone numbers, and the promises to keep in touch – 'Cross my heart and hope to die' – that would not be kept. As Grandpa closed the boot and edged the car forwards, Arthur waved at the familiar faces pressing at the windows. He wondered if this was how a convict felt on the day of release – a mixture of relief, hope, anxiety and even sadness. Friends and enemies, routines, however tiresome, and everything familiar were being left behind. Now even Sparrowhawk's hardships seemed to have been a comfort and support.

*

Arthur looks down at the photograph of himself with his Sparrowhawk chums, each pulling a gleeful face: a disparate band of brothers who had stuck together and thrived in a loveless place. Only rarely, in all the years since, has he thought about what happened to them after that end of term. For him, they are boys who never grew up. He looks at the caption beneath and, as he does so, hears again the reading of the register: 'Barnes, Belcher, Bingham, Bowler, Bowring, Bright'.

Alice knocks softly and comes in to pick up the tea things. Arthur is asleep in his chair, his breathing soft and steady, and his book has slipped to the floor. She picks it up and puts it carefully on the table. It is still open at the photograph of young Arthur and his friends (she recognizes Arthur on the right), and she can't help smiling. A feisty and mischievous crew. Where are the others now, she muses, and what are their stories? And for how long will Arthur be able to remember them?

II

Mary

Of course, in spite of Arthur's unprompted denial, something did happen with Sarah, and not only does he remember it, but after more than sixty years it still leaps out and ambushes him at unexpected moments. Like his mother's death and his time at Sparrowhawk Hall, it would shape the person he became. Some time afterwards there would also be an embarrassing coda, which might have had devastating consequences, but in the end did not. It is not mentioned in Arthur's book, because only he and Sarah ever knew about it and to what it led, and neither would ever tell. Grandpa probably guessed what had happened and perhaps Mrs Jones guessed too, although, if she did, she had the good sense to keep it to herself; and they are both long since dead.

It was in July, just after Arthur had left Sparrowhawk. Over the four years he had been away at school, he had come to feel like an outsider in Hartbourne. His village friends had grown up without him, moved on to one of the schools in Grantham, formed new alliances, learned more about life than the time-warped isolation of Sparrowhawk could ever teach, become more worldly-wise. Occasionally, during the school holidays, he had met up with Norman: they had gone cycling together or taken the rackety 54 bus into Grantham and wandered round the shops or the Saturday market; or, as in the old days, there had been a sleepover at the cottage, but the spark between them had all but disappeared. And from time to time, encouraged by Grandpa and Grandma, who grew tired of his sitting around the house, Arthur had got together with Sarah. Taking one of Grandma's legendary picnics as a bribe, they would go for reluctant walks in the surrounding countryside.

Although Arthur and Sarah had always been neighbours, as children theirs had been a distant relationship: they had had little in common and had never been that close. Now, however, they were both teenagers and things had started to change. To everyone who knew them, they seemed an unlikely twosome: Sarah had grown from the plump ugly duckling in the school photograph into a graceful and confident swan, while Arthur, for all his Sparrowhawk swagger, remained underneath an anxious and self-conscious schoolboy with the rather prim old-fashioned manner and dress which came from living with his grandparents. But, as hormones stirred, the magnets which had once repelled began to attract. Now Arthur was captivated by Sarah's long blond hair and her come-hither eyes, and that morning he could not take his eyes off the not-quite-developed breasts which showed through her cotton dress. She noticed and enjoyed the attention. As they walked along, she teased and flirted with him, and he had no idea how to react.

They picnicked in their usual spot, a shadowy grove a little way from the footpath, with views across the chequerboard fields to the distant hills. Like Galleons Lap, thought Arthur, at the end of *The House at Pooh Corner*, where Christopher Robin says goodbye to Pooh for ever. Rabbits hopped close by and a hawk hovered in the cloudless sky, watching and waiting. For some reason, it felt different there today – a place where time didn't matter and the turning world slowed and stopped. They sat in silence, sensing some sort of charge sparking between them, until Arthur, half wanting to break the spell, rummaged in his rucksack for his *Schoolboys' Guide to British Birds* and tried to work out whether it was a buzzard or a kestrel he could see above them.

'We're moving away, Arthur,' said Sarah suddenly.

Arthur looked up. 'What do you mean? Moving away where?'

'Dad's got a new job near London. We're leaving next month.'

'You can't.' Arthur's voice was cracking with emotion. He was already missing Sparrowhawk terribly, and now this. 'You've always been here, next door.'

'I don't want to go either,' said Sarah, standing up, 'It's crap, but there's nothing I can do about it, is there? I'm going to miss you all like crazy.'

'You'll make new friends.' Arthur sounded more jealous than comforting. He went back to his book, but the words were blurred and he wasn't reading them anyway. There was a long and uneasy silence.

Then, 'Arthur,' whispered Sarah. Arthur looked up. She had peeled off her dress and stood naked in front of him. 'There,' she said, 'that's what you've been wanting to see all morning, isn't it?'

Arthur blushed as much as it is possible to blush. 'I'm sorry,' he said. 'I didn't mean ...'

'Don't be sorry,' smiled Sarah. 'It's all right. We're friends, aren't we?'

Arthur did not know whether to look or not. He had never seen a girl like this. The curves of her body were nothing like a boy's, her skin was white and smooth like newly fallen snow, and between her legs was a darkness that enthralled him. For some reason he felt only a sense of shame. Eating the forbidden fruit.

Sarah moved towards him. 'Come on, Arthur,' she said. 'Fair's fair. My turn now. And already she was unbuttoning his shorts and easing them down.

Arthur did nothing to stop her. He felt himself stirring and growing, and he looked away in embarrassment. He could only think of one of the rude schoolboy rhymes they had told each other at Sparrowhawk when none of the masters was about, but it wasn't funny anymore:

> *My friend Billy had a ten-foot willy*
> *And he showed it to the girl next door.*
> *She thought it was a snake and hit it with a rake*
> *And now it's only two foot four.*

'I don't think we ought …' he stammered, but already Sarah had reached out and grasped him and was moving her hand up and down, up and down. More than nearly anything, Arthur wanted her to stop, but more than anything he wanted her to carry on. Up and down, slow then fast. He closed his eyes tight and was thrilled and scared by the new and strange sensations that built and built until they made him cry out and for a few seconds overwhelmed him. He lay on the ground for a while, exhausted and appalled, and when at last he opened his eyes Sarah was smiling at him knowingly. She had put her dress back on. 'You enjoyed that, didn't you, Arthur?' she said, a note of triumph in her voice. 'Come on, tidy yourself up. You never know who might come along.'

Arthur said nothing. He was just relieved that no-one had come along already. What would have happened if they'd been caught? He hitched up his shorts, hauled himself up slowly and brushed the sun-parched grass from his clothes. Sarah stood there waiting as if nothing had happened.

Arthur watched the light playing through her dress. 'But why,' he asked, if you're going away …?'

Sarah laughed. 'Call it a leaving present'; and then, more seriously, 'You must promise not to tell, Arthur, or we'll both be in terrible trouble. If anyone asks, you must say that nothing happened.'

So they began to walk slowly back to the village. They were closer than they had ever been, but a gulf had opened between them. Sarah led the way; Arthur trailed behind her. Neither of them spoke. There were no words to describe or disguise Arthur's confusion. Then, 'Don't go, Sarah,' he pleaded uselessly.

'You know I don't have a choice, Arthur. And we'll keep in touch, and I'm sure I'll come back to see you all. I can always stay with Aunt Dorothy.'

Arthur didn't like the 'all'. It was as if, even after today, he wasn't special. He suspected she had done this before with someone else. Probably more than once.

When at last they reached the road, Arthur felt the few people they passed were staring at them accusingly and now Mrs Jones was walking briskly towards them with Alfie, her neatly coiffed poodle, following proudly in her wake. 'Hello, you two,' she greeted them. 'What have you been up to? Enjoying this glorious weather?'

'Hello, Mrs Jones,' said Sarah. 'Yes, it's a lovely day, isn't it? We've been out for one of our picnics.'

Alfie sniffed Arthur's shorts. 'Don't be so rude, Alfie,' said Mrs Jones and pulled him away.

Arthur looked at the ground. She knows, he thought, and so does Alfie. He can smell it.

'Don't look so glum, Arthur,' chided Mrs Jones. 'It's not at all like you. What's the matter? Too much picnic?'

'It's nothing, Mrs Jones,' mumbled Arthur. He was blushing again.

Mrs Jones was wise enough to know that 'nothing' meant 'something', but it was none of her business anymore and with a cheery goodbye she went on her way. 'What was all that blushing about, Arthur?' hissed Sarah. 'You'll give us both away.'

The 'For Sale' sign which had been put up in front of Sarah's house while they were out confirmed what Sarah had said. Arthur was despondent that evening and ate hardly any of his supper. 'Is there something wrong with you, Arthur?' asked Grandma. 'That was one of your favourites.'

'Sarah's going away,' said Arthur, but he would not look at her.

'I know. It's a shame, isn't it, but she's never been a particular friend of yours.'

'Yes, she has,' snapped Arthur. Still he would not look at her.

Angrily, he pushed back his chair, ran upstairs to his room, banged the door.

'Oh dear, that's not like Arthur at all,' said Grandma as she made to follow him.

'I'd leave him, if I were you,' said Grandpa. 'He'll get over it soon enough.'

'I know Sarah's always been there, and we'll miss all of them. But I didn't think he really cared about her.'

'Then you haven't noticed much since he's been back from school this time.'

'Noticed what?'

'First bite at the apple, I guess,' said Grandpa, remembering back to his own youth with a twinge of regret.

'What on earth do you mean by that?'

But Grandpa, with a faraway look in his eyes, pretended not to hear. He began absent-mindedly to clear the plates.

*

'Don't you want to go for another walk with Sarah?' asked Grandpa, when Arthur was mooching round the house doing nothing in particular. 'It would do you good to get out and Grandma will always make you a picnic.'

'I'm not fussed,' said Arthur. 'I'll go sometime.' He was fussed and wanted desperately to go for another walk, but he dared not ask her.

'Well, they'll be moving soon, so don't miss your chance.'

Arthur carried on reading. He wanted Sarah to be the one to ask. And one morning, shortly before the summer holiday ended, there was a knock at the door which Grandpa answered. Arthur listened and his heart leapt. 'I'm just going into town and wondered if Arthur wanted to come too,' said Sarah. She was wearing a modest turquoise tee shirt and denim shorts.

'I'm sure he'd love to,' said Grandpa. 'But come along in and ask him yourself.' He called upstairs: 'Arthur, it's Sarah for you.'

Arthur could not believe his luck and bounded down into the hall. 'Hi, Arthur,' said Sarah. 'I'm getting the bus into Grantham for a last look round and I hoped you'd come with me. We could grab a burger at the Wimpy Bar.'

'You bet! Just let me get some shoes. It's all right, isn't it, Grandpa?' Some minutes later he reappeared in different and smarter clothes.

'Very fetching,' said Sarah. Arthur wished he could stop blushing. 'Come on, then.'

'You'll need some money for lunch for you and your lady,' said Grandpa and handed him a pound note.

He knows too, thought Arthur. 'Thanks, Grandpa,' he said, as they headed off. Grandpa watched as they walked to the bus stop uneasily apart.

*

As the bus rattled along, Arthur and Sarah sat largely in silence. In Grantham they went straight to the Wimpy Bar and ordered Whippsy milk shakes and burgers and chips. 'I'm really sorry about when we had a picnic,' said Sarah in a matter-of-fact way. 'I didn't know you hadn't ...'

Arthur's face reddened. 'It doesn't matter. And nothing happened, did it?' And they grinned at each other, and the air had been cleared enough, and they talked about other things – about Sparrowhawk and the new school far away from Hartbourne where Arthur would go in September; about where Sarah was moving to and her own new school ('All girls and posh,' she complained, although Arthur thought 'all girls' might be safer for everyone); and about lots of stuff that wasn't important at all. Then, as a sort of present to each other, they shared a high-as-the-sky knickerbocker glory, a glorious mélange of ice cream, fruit cocktail, strawberry sauce and cream, topped with a chocolate flake and served in the tallest of glasses with two long-handled spoons.

'You will write, won't you?' said Arthur as they got up to go.

'Of course. Promise.' Arthur was covered in confusion when she took his hand.

At the end of the day they said goodbye at Sarah's garden gate. Sarah kissed Arthur hard on the lips (which still tasted vaguely of knickerbocker glory) and was surprised when he responded in kind. Another hug, and then she turned, walked up the path and, with a final wave, went inside. It was all a bit syrupy, she decided, like in a romantic novel. Even so, she wondered if Arthur was a bit more special than the other boys she'd toyed with. If only he were a bit older. He needed to grow up.

As for Arthur, he was both elated and distraught. Sarah had opened a door, albeit frighteningly, and fate had all but slammed it shut. First love, the best and the worst, and waiting for the promised letters that would never come.

*

At Marsh View, the days crawl by. The birds peck at the feeder. People come to see Arthur. Sometimes it is Alice; sometimes they are carers he hardly recognises, always well-meaning, thank goodness, but often patronising. At Sparrowhawk, and later at the Burgoyne School, he was Bright, not Arthur, a stripping of identity; here he is 'Love' or 'Darling'. Meaningless words, he thinks: everyone at Marsh View is 'Love' or 'Darling'. Another stripping. 'I am Arthur', he wants to say, but doesn't. From time to time, Flo and Maria visit him, and his face lights up. He knows they are his daughters, but he cannot relate them to the little girls he remembers more clearly, and within a few minutes of their leaving he has forgotten they have been. Often he worries about his mother. He must go to see her. She died nearly seventy years ago; she would be over a hundred if she were alive.

I Am Arthur Bright

Today, when Alice brings Arthur his morning coffee, he is looking in his book at the photograph of the village school. He smiles at her. 'Are you … Sarah?'

'No, Arthur. I'm Alice.'

Arthur thinks for a bit. 'Alice … in wonderland?'

'That's right, Arthur. Alice in wonderland.'

Arthur looks back at the photograph, points at Sarah with his finger, turns the page. There is the photograph of him with his friends at Sparrowhawk Hall: Barnes, Belcher, Bingham, Bowler, Bowring and Bright. He pauses, turns the page again. Here there is a photograph of teenage Arthur in a military uniform. 'That's a very smart uniform you're wearing, Arthur,' says Alice, as she has said so many times. 'Were you a soldier?'

Arthur shakes his head. 'No, not a soldier.'

The Burgoyne School, where the photograph was taken, had been recommended to Grandpa and Grandma by Mr Cholmondeley-Robinson because it offered help to boys who had lost their fathers in military service. It had begun life as The Burgoyne Boys' Home for the sons of men who had died in the Crimean War and even in the 1950s, by when it had become a minor public school, it continued to run on harsh military lines. Grandpa and Grandma had always planned for Arthur to come back home and go to the grammar school in Hartbourne, but then they had decided it would be better for him to be surrounded by boys of his own age and to benefit from all kinds of activities which at their age they could not offer.

Arthur knew Grandpa and Grandma only wanted the best for him, and were paying fees they could barely afford, so he never told them how unhappy he was at Burgoyne and unhappily they never noticed. He hated its militarism – the polishing of belts and boots, the afternoons spent marching, the Sunday parades, the rigours of the assault course, and the time spent firing and cleaning rifles. Many of the masters were former servicemen and bore the scars to show it

– sometimes etched in their flesh, sometimes in the way they walked, sometimes in their sudden bursts of anger, sometimes in the way they drank to forget – and he wondered what they really felt about Burgoyne. He hated the way the whole architecture and artefacts of the school, and its attitudes and language, reflected the absurd values of the crumbling Empire. And more than anything he hated the whole gung-ho glorification of war. He had never stopped being proud of his father, but neither had he stopped resenting the way he had died, cannon-fodder on the shores of France, and the way all his mother's hopes had been mown down with him. He was not a coward and if there were another war he would join up with everyone else, but treating war as a game – throwing thunder-flashes and bayoneting dummies – simply turned his stomach.

Although Arthur was naturally diffident, he made no secret of his contempt for Burgoyne and all it stood for, and consequently he came in for a deal of bullying. There was the initiation, when they pulled down his trousers and smeared black boot polish on his privates – 'Black balls! Black balls!'; there was water poured into his bed, night after night – 'Look, Arthur's peed himself again'; there was, once, excrement smeared in his clean underpants – 'Poo boy! Poo boy!'; there were the sly kicks and punches; in rugby games, there were boot studs carved down his shin; there were the names – 'Mummy's boy' was the one that hurt the most. But he buried himself in his studies, found frequent refuge in the seldom used school library, and told no-one. He was beaten only once, when, engrossed in a book, he had failed to support the school team: there were four strokes of the cane and, because he refused to cry, there was a fifth. More than pain, he felt humiliated, and angry at the pointlessness of it all.

Only two people at Burgoyne showed any interest in Arthur. The young history master, the nicely named Mr Castle, perhaps showed too much interest, although it was never apparent or explicit. He guided Arthur's reading, talked through his essays, offered the occasional coffee or surreptitious glass of beer. It was Mr Castle who, like Mr Penfold at Sparrowhawk, encouraged Arthur's love of the subject and inspired him to become a teacher one day himself. The English master, Dr Robinson, balding, dour and wise, introduced him to the whole gamut of English literature; he made him learn poems by heart and in years to come even Alzheimer's could not steal them away. Not surprisingly, Flo and Maria included none of this: they had found only a handful of Burgoyne photographs and some end-of-term reports which damned with faint and sneering praise ('Bright is a talented boy and is always diligent in his studies, but he contributes little to the community and as a consequence has made few friends here. He has been a member of the chapel choir.'). There was nothing else to show Arthur had been at The Burgoyne School at all.

However, for all Arthur's misery, the ill wind which drove him to take refuge in his books also swept him to examination success. Although he would have been welcomed at either Oxford or Cambridge, in a small act of rebellion he chose instead to apply for one of the new universities that were springing up in England in the 1960s. The headmaster had urged Arthur to redeem himself by adding his name to Burgoyne's sparsely populated Oxbridge Honours Board, but yet again he was disappointed in his quietly defiant pupil.

*

In 1963, the University of Norfolk was still under construction in a muted brick on the not yet fashionable North Norfolk coast. One day it would stand majestically as a buttress against the penetrating winter winds, but in those early days much of the teaching and accommodation was in prefabricated cabins which, in times of storm, would strain and rock like ships riding uneasily at anchor. It was situated a little way from the sea and on a clear day the waves could be seen spitting or sparkling beyond the reed beds, the marshes and the winding creeks. To travel there from Hartbourne meant catching a series of trains which moved crab-like across the increasingly flat and featureless landscape, and then, at the terminus at Hunstanton, there was an infrequent bus for the last part of the journey. To study there was to make a statement of self-sufficiency, of not wanting to be one of the crowd (although that was never its intention and, as it expanded, would not last). For Arthur, it was also a statement of individuality and independence, a much-needed antidote to the numbing conformity of Burgoyne.

*

Another slow day at Marsh View: the blue tits at the feeder; a wisp of wind rustling the springtime leaves; Arthur's book lying open on his knee. 'Is that Mary?' asks Alice.

Arthur peers at the photograph of a dark-haired girl in a 1960s fit-and-flare dress and kitten heels. She is grinning mischievously at the camera. 'Yes ... that's Mary,' he says slowly. Haltingly he reads the words beneath: 'I first met ... Mary at the University ... of Norfolk.'

'You married Mary, didn't you?'

Arthur looks puzzled. 'I think so,' he says at last, although he does not seem sure. More than half a century of marriage has somehow slipped away, but Arthur's first meeting with Mary is another memory that has clung on. Flo and Maria had heard Mum and Dad tell of it many times and it is a shame they recorded none of the detail in Arthur's *Story*. Maybe they did not consider it important.

Arthur had been on the final leg of his journey to university and he could not help noticing the girl who boarded the bus in front of him. She was quite tall; her features were soft – a slightly retroussé nose and a wide, generous mouth; she had dark, shoulder-length hair and amazing, dream-deep eyes. Arthur reckoned she was another student, although she was confident enough not to be a fresher like him. He wanted to move next to her and to strike up a conversation, but he lacked the courage and anyway she was engrossed in a magazine. When at last the bus stopped at the University, Arthur stood up and clambered off with his luggage. The girl smiled at him, but she made no attempt to move and his hope of making a new friend was dashed.

The first few days of university were a disappointment for Arthur. He doubted if he'd been right to come to this not yet flourishing place and he spent too much time in his room. He went shopping for a few basic provisions and made his first clumsy attempts in the communal kitchen to cook for himself. Some evenings he sat alone in the Union bar and drank too much. He walked the paths that led to the marshy wilderness and began to feel at one with the vast expanse of wetland, sea and sky. At the end of the week, he visited the freshers' 'Societies Fair' and realised he wasn't interested in very much. There were political clubs, but he had no particular political allegiance; there were religious groups, but although religion had been a daily ritual at Sparrowhawk and Burgoyne, he hadn't been wholly convinced, and he studiously ignored the various evangelical blandishments; he wasn't a sportsman – the obsession with competitive sport at Burgoyne was another thing that had turned him off; he wasn't a musician either. He was nearly tempted by the Naturalists, but it was the solitude of the marshes which attracted him and that would be spoiled by the company of others. He joined the History Society because he thought it was the right thing to do – after all, he was here to study history for three years. Then, as he turned to leave, he saw beside the 'Dram Soc' banner the girl from the bus. She was wearing a dark green, floaty, ankle-length dress and she smiled at him in half-recognition – a siren smile – and, without thinking, he made the mistake of going over to the table.

'Hello there! You were on the bus last week, weren't you? How are you settling in?'

'I'm beginning to get used to it,' said Arthur, not very truthfully.

'Good for you! I hated my first week, but once the teaching starts and you get to know people, it does get better.'

Arthur did not look reassured.

'Are you interested in drama?'

'No, not ... I mean, yes, a bit ...'

'You ought to join us. You'd meet lots of people. We're putting on *Oedipus Rex* this term. It's going to be fun.'

'Fun' wasn't a word that Arthur would use to describe *Oedipus Rex*. He didn't know much about plays, but thanks to Dr Robinson he knew *Oedipus* was about incest, murder, suicide and gouged-out eyes. However, fun seemed exactly the right word for the girl with the smile, the dream-deep eyes and, he now noticed, the slightly husky voice. 'I've never done much acting,' he said.

'Oh, that doesn't matter. We've cast the main parts, and I'm playing Jocasta, Oedipus's wife, but we still need loads of people in the Chorus. Do join us. I know you'd enjoy it.'

'All right.' Arthur was not very enthusiastic. He was not keen on either the play or the Chorus, and 'Dram Soc' sounded twee and pretentious, but it would mean he could meet the girl again.

'That's great. You won't regret it, I promise. I'm Mary, by the way. I just can't wait.'

'I'm Arthur.' He was just wondering if he should shake her hand, when she gave him a hug instead. He blushed.

'There's everything about auditions and rehearsals on the Union noticeboard. First ones are next week. We'll see you then.' Already Mary was turning her attention to another unwary fresher and Arthur felt a pang of jealousy. That afternoon, as he walked again towards the marshes, he could not stop thinking about her.

*

To Arthur's disappointment, the main characters and the Chorus were split for the first few rehearsals, so it was a whole month before he met up with Mary again. Even then, she was always deep in conversation with the play's director or with the student playing Oedipus and there was little opportunity to talk to her. He wasn't enjoying acting and, since Mary was apparently ignoring him, he could see he had made a stupid mistake. Of course a bubbly second-year would have no interest in a naive and insecure fresher. What had he been thinking? Only his pride kept him from dropping out.

The play ran for three nights at the beginning of December and even Arthur was entranced by the magic of performance. The scenery, the costumes, the lights, and the audiences, swept away the tedium of learning lines and moves, and brought everything to life. The hall quietened. Thebes was caught in a rising tide of plague and death. Oedipus addressed the frightened citizens and Creon, his brother-in-law, returned from the house of Apollo with the demand for purification of the city, the payment of blood for blood. And now it was the turn of the Chorus to speak, voices rising and pleading in unison. Arthur, as he realised afterwards, lost all his inhibitions and was, for the first time, caught up in the action. Like the rest of the citizens, he was desperate to know what would happen, although in reality he knew exactly how the plot would unfold. When Mary entered as Jocasta, her hair piled imperiously high, he found it impossible to take his eyes off her: how could she, in life so unassuming, transform herself into someone so different and so powerful? Irrationally he wanted to shout she was not to blame for her unknowing incest, and when the Attendant brought news of Jocasta's death, he could not separate her from Mary and was overcome by grief.

On the final night, after the lights had dimmed and the audience had drifted away, the cast retired to the Union bar. There was a noisy, beer-fuelled hubbub, mutual congratulations and backslapping, tales of lines forgotten and disasters averted, delight in success and a feeling of emptiness now it had come to an end. Arthur, who was not sure how he fitted into all this, looked with childish hope for Mary in the crowd and caught sight of her moving towards the door. He summoned up his Dutch courage and walked over to her. 'Hi Mary. You were fantastic. And I have to admit you were right, I did enjoy it in the end. Won't you stay for another drink?'

'Thanks, Arthur, but I'm tired. And I'm not into all this luvvy stuff.' She flashed her engaging smile.

Without really meaning to, Arthur found himself leaving with Mary. Somewhat to her surprise, she did nothing to dissuade him. He didn't seem her type at all, but he was intriguing: tall and slim, mouse-coloured hair, blue eyes, pale complexion tanned a little by the wind, conservatively dressed, ordinary. Not needy, but vulnerable. Not quite out of his depth, but a loner – although perhaps he didn't want to be? Not confident, but, in a strange way, single-minded. Closed in. Safe. So when he suggested, nervously, a drink somewhere else, 'Oh, why not, Arthur? That'd be nice,' she said, with that same engaging smile.

In fact, they were both hungry, so as well as a drink at the King's Head they splashed out on sausage, chips and beans. Arthur insisted on paying. They talked of this and that. Mary discovered something of Arthur's childhood and his boarding school experiences – which explained a lot. Arthur learnt of Mary's conventional middle-class upbringing – in Lincoln, not that far from Hartbourne: she, too, was an only child and was glad to have the chance at university to strike out on her own. She was studying fine art. 'I chose Norfolk because it's not overwhelming. There are lots of opportunities, like doing plays, and I probably wouldn't get a look-in at somewhere bigger.'

Before long, 'last orders' were called and Arthur walked Mary home – a room in a student house in the nearby village, overlooking the sea. She did not invite him in. She gave him a friendly hug and a quick kiss on the cheek, and she was gone. He strolled back to the campus with that hollow feeling in his stomach. He had no idea what Mary thought of him, but the next day there was a Christmas card nestling in his pigeon-hole: 'Thanks for supper and walking me home last night, Arthur. Have a good Christmas. Look forward to seeing you next term. Love, Mary xx.'

His heart leapt: 'Love, Mary xx.'

*

In January there are few places in England colder than the Norfolk coast and Arthur hardly recognised Mary wrapped up in a bright red scarf and woolly hat when they met one morning on the university walkway.

'Arthur! How are you doing? Did you have a good Christmas?'

'Not bad, thanks. But it's good to be back.' And, bravely, 'Time for a coffee?'

'That'd be lovely, Arthur. I need something to warm me up. But it'll have to be quick. I've got a lecture at midday.'

It was the first time Mary had been to Arthur's room. It was identical to the one she had had the year before – white walls and a dark blue carpet, a built-in bed with drawers under, a desk and chair, a bookshelf, a modern easy chair (more style than comfort), a brown cork noticeboard, a wardrobe, a washbasin. 'Make yourself at home,' said Arthur, moving some essay notes from the easy chair. 'I'll just go and make the coffee. Won't be a moment.'

He returned a few minutes later with two mugs of coffee and a packet of biscuits.

'Wow! Chocolate digestives! A real treat!'

'Grandma always packs me off with a box of supplies. She still insists on spoiling me.'

They swapped stories of Christmas. Always the same, the same, with turkey and trimmings, the Queen's speech, a walk in the rain through half-deserted streets, Morecambe and Wise, and not much else to do.

Then Mary changed the subject. 'I so wanted to meet up with you, Arthur, and wasn't sure where your room was. You see, they're letting me direct a play this term. It's *The Chairs* by Ionesco. I'm sure you've heard of it.'

Arthur shook his head. 'I'm afraid not. I'm not very well-up on plays. What's it about?'

Mary thought for a bit. 'Well ... there are two old people who talk to an audience that isn't there, and an invisible Emperor, and an orator who can't speak. At the end the oldies jump into the sea and drown themselves.'

'It all sounds a bit mad.'

'I suppose that's the point. It's about life being absurd. ... Anyway, I'm still trying to get my head round it. But I want someone to help me with it, Arthur, and I thought of you.'

Arthur didn't know how to answer. It would mean spending time with Mary, which he wanted more than anything, and it was just possible she wanted to be with him, too: there were plenty of more suitable people she could have asked. But he knew he wasn't cut out for the stage. 'I'm just not sure,' he said. 'I suppose I enjoyed *Oedipus* in the end, but it proved I'm pretty rubbish at acting.'

'You weren't rubbish, Arthur, but I wasn't actually thinking of you acting, and anyway I've already cast the two main parts. No, I thought you could be a sort of stage manager. There's so much I won't have time for. And I need some moral support.' She paused, before making another suggestion. 'Of course, you could be the Orator right at the end if you want. He doesn't have to say anything.'

'Thanks a bunch.'

'Oh, I didn't mean it like that. But you will help me, Arthur, won't you? ... I'd really like it to be you.'

Gallantly, Arthur agreed. He was flattered that Mary had asked him and not anyone else, and faint heart never won fair lady, did it?

What else could he have done?

*

Arthur's spring term, like Ionesco's stage, was filled with *Chairs* – so much so that his history assignments were not as good as before. He did, in fact, have quite enough time for studying, but his mind was elsewhere. It was partly filled with the play, partly with a new-found interest in drama, and mainly with Mary. On most days she would drop into his room with another idea; sometimes they would have lunch together; sometimes she would join him on a marsh walk and he would point out the different plants and birds; and sometimes, of an evening, they would retreat from the cold and sit together in front of the fire in the King's Head. They enjoyed each other's company.

As the week of the performance approached, Arthur went along to all the rehearsals and made notes of what would be needed. There were props and lights to be organised, and chairs to be rounded up. With three weeks to go, Mary arrived at Arthur's room with the question he had been expecting and dreading: 'You will play the Orator, won't you, Arthur? It's just up your street.'

Arthur hesitated. In the *Oedipus* Chorus he'd been largely invisible, but this would be altogether different. 'I don't reckon I could be the stage manager and the Orator. It just wouldn't work.'

'But it would, Arthur. Once the play begins, there won't be a lot of stage-managing for you to do. And you understand it better than anyone. There's a fabulous costume and you'll only have to look miserable and grunt.' Mary smiled – the smile that always disarmed him. She knew he would do it.

Arthur discovered too late that the Orator had much more to do than grunt: there was a fair amount of stage business, which he just about mastered after days of practising. And he didn't care for the 'fabulous costume' – a large black felt hat, an artist's blouse, a bow tie, a moustache, and a beard – but in spite of his misgivings he rather stole the show. After the final performance, Mary and Arthur escaped as soon as they could to the King's Head, where they mulled over the production ('You were great, Arthur – no, don't say anything!'); then, in the drizzly March rain, they walked back to Mary's place, a large bed-sit which she had decorated with vibrant posters and her own quirky artwork. They shared a bottle of cheap red wine and talked of many things – of *The Chairs*, of the University, and of Mary's departure in September for the year in Florence which was part of her fine art degree. For Mary it was an enticing prospect – it was one of the features that had attracted her to the course – although she would miss Arthur, to whom she had grown close over the past few months. Arthur knew he would be bereft, but he did not admit it. He found it hard to make friends and Mary had helped to lift his spirits. She made him feel important. He had no doubt that he was in love.

It was well past midnight when Arthur stood up to go and the drizzle had turned into heavy rain. He would be soaked, but it had been a good evening and it was worth getting wet. But, 'You can't go out in that, Arthur,' said Mary. 'Why don't you stay the night?' He was covered in confusion. His face reddened. He thought of the picnic with Sarah. 'Oh, don't look so worried, I'm not going to eat you. I didn't mean sleep with me. Not yet anyway. The sofa's not that uncomfortable and I've got some blankets you can use.'

'I didn't think …,' said Arthur. He had thought, of course, and was both relieved and bitterly disappointed. It was not long before he curled up on the sofa under the blankets and lay for a while wondering what Mary had meant by 'Not yet'. Then, under the dulling effect of the wine, he fell into a contented slumber.

Spring gave way to summer and Arthur and Mary forsook the theatre. Arthur turned his mind back to his neglected studies, revising for his preliminary exams, while Mary busied herself with the groundwork for her project in Florence, but they still found time to walk through the wetlands and sometimes, at weekends and using the infrequent local buses, they explored further along the coast. Eventually, after one especially enjoyable outing, they did sleep together, clumsily. It was the first time for both of them — more rite of passage than bower of bliss, they reflected laughingly as they breakfasted together the next morning; but before long they were making love without embarrassment and it felt entirely right.

Over the long summer vacation, Mary and Arthur lived in Mary's bedsit, taking the chance to visit some of Norfolk's great houses and photographing the breathtaking sea lavender on the marshes, but with the growing awareness that Mary would soon be leaving for her Italian adventure and the idyll would come to an end. In the last week of August, they packed up Mary's belongings and her parents drove down to collect her for a few days at home before taking her to the airport, while Arthur made the zigzag journey back to Grandpa and Grandma. He tried hard to be cheerful, but he found their naturally interested questions intrusive. For some reason he didn't want to tell them about Mary — perhaps because he feared it might all be over — and they would have been shocked if it came out they had been living as a couple. Not even Grandma's sumptuous meals could lift his spirits. He knew he was behaving unreasonably, but he was too dejected to do anything about it. Unsurprisingly, Grandpa and Grandma worried about him. Was everything all right at university?

Thus Arthur spent his second-year immersed in his books and in due course he would ascribe his first-class degree to Mary's absence. He helped out backstage with a couple of theatre productions, though with little enjoyment, and he spent more time on the marshes, watching as autumn turned to winter and winter to spring. In November, the teal, the widgeon, and the pink-footed geese arrived for their winter sojourn and flew off again in March, and on the mudflats the wading birds came from the Arctic for their seasonal break. Each week Arthur wrote a blue airmail letter to Mary and each week he received a letter in return, which made him envious of the busy social life she appeared to be leading. He imagined the worst, but dared not ask if her feelings towards him had changed. Once she sent him photographs, one taken outside the famous basilica of Santa Maria del Fiore, one with a group of students on the Ponte Vecchio with its myriad shops, one in front of a vegetable stall in the crowded market at San Lorenzo, and one sitting with friends outside a smart restaurant on the Piazza del Duomo. She looked happy, but he noticed how one good-looking male student, stylishly dressed and sporting a fashionable 'Beatles' haircut, was always next to her.

Arthur spent Christmas with Grandpa and Grandma, and when on Christmas evening there was a telephone call from Italy they understood at last what was going on. Now he had spoken to Mary, he felt reassured and remained cheerful until he travelled back to Norfolk in the New Year. Over the coming months her letters became less newsy and more about them and what they might do when she returned, and if sometimes he woke in the early hours and was wracked with doubt, he was on the whole more assured and relaxed. When in June Mary finally returned, Arthur noticed how she was no longer just an undergraduate but a young woman as well. And Mary saw that Arthur had shed his naivety: he had lost none of his wry sense of humour, but now there were a new depth and seriousness. For three days in a row they walked the sunlit marsh paths, recounting all that had happened to each of them, sometimes lapsing into happy silence, and soon turning their minds to the future. 'I loved Florence,' said Mary, 'and one day we're going to go back there together.'

That summer, Arthur took Mary to stay with Grandpa and Grandma, who thoroughly approved (Mary was, of course, given a separate room), and Mary took Arthur to meet her own more liberal parents. 'Not the dashing young man I'd expected,' said her father, although he was rather portly and far from dashing himself, 'but he's intelligent and reliable, I suppose.'

'He's much more than that,' said Mary's mother, who was as unpretentious as her daughter. 'I like him a lot and they're just right for each other. I do hope it will last.'

*

After her sojourn in Florence, Mary was eager to get out into the world and found it difficult to return to the ordinariness of university life. She took a room on campus to be close to the library and to Arthur. They were happy each to have their own space for working – 'finals' had become the inevitable focus – but their domestic arrangements remained much as before. Although accommodation was in separate blocks for men and women, and overnight liaisons were officially forbidden, the porters chose only to notice the most flagrant of breaches.

One morning, after collecting the mail, Mary waved a letter at Arthur. 'It's from Ray, one of the guys I met in Florence. He wants to come and visit. You don't mind, do you? I can't wait to see him again.'

Arthur's heart sank. 'I suppose he's the wannabe Beatle who's cuddling up to you in all the photographs?' His nonchalance could not disguise his dismay.

'Probably! He was jolly nice. And very rich. We did a lot of things together.'

Arthur said nothing. His life was being knocked off course.

'Oh, Arthur, don't be so stupid. There's nothing for you to worry about. I told Ray all about us. As Mum would say, he bats outrageously for the other side. He was just great to be with.'

'Well, I suppose …' Arthur was a little mollified. 'But where would he stay?'

'At the King's Head, I should think. He's got pots of money, after all. I'd really like you to meet him.'

So one weekend Ray came, fashionable and flamboyant, in his

MGB sports car, and stayed at the King's Head for a couple of days, and twice treated Arthur and Mary to dinner. He was intrigued by the half-built university. He walked with them through the marshes, although his smart white trainers were hardly appropriate, and, with Mary contorted in the back, drove them to all their favourite places. Arthur was defensive at first, but once he saw there was no threat, and Ray was both intelligent and amusing, he quickly mellowed. In time they would become the closest of friends. 'Thank you, Arthur,' said Mary. 'He wasn't so bad, was he?'

*

At Marsh View, Arthur's attention has wandered, but Alice is looking through the photographs. She has seen them many times before, but she is always intrigued by these glimpses into Arthur's past, a young man with life rolling out in front of him. There is a photograph of Mary as Jocasta, with Arthur just visible in the Chorus, one of Arthur as the Orator in *The Chairs* (the outrageous costume makes Alice laugh out loud), and one of both Arthur and Mary taken professionally at the 1966 Graduation Ball. Arthur is in a dinner suit (hired for the occasion); Mary looks stunning in a daringly cut indigo ball gown. Their industry had paid off and both had achieved first-class honours. Alice touches Arthur's sleeve. 'That's a gorgeous photograph, Arthur. Do you remember that evening? It must have been very special.'

And, yes, it is another of the moments Arthur does just about remember. It was late June, and for once in that dismal summer the air was warm and still. There had been a formal dinner in the refectory and a large marquee had been set up on the university lawn. Arthur and Mary had danced most of the night away, but when the music became louder and the atmosphere unruly, they retreated outside. The big Norfolk sky was clear and the stars seemed unusually bright. There was one star which shone brighter than the others.

'Look, that's our star, Arthur,' said Mary, and she reached up and kissed him. For a while they stood in silence. They could hear the disco playing 'Save the last dance for me' and, far off, the contented susurration of the sea, and they were conscious that this chapter in their lives was almost over. Arthur thought of his mother, and of Sparrowhawk Hall, and of The Burgoyne School, and of how, here, in Norfolk, he had experienced a new sort of happiness, and that was because of Mary. 'Mary,' he said, although he had not meant to say it now.

'Yes?'

'Would you …' and Arthur stopped, because he did not know how to phrase it, and he did not want it to come out wrong.

'Of course,' said Mary, 'I thought you'd never ask,' and she kissed him again.

III

Afloat

After the giddy emotions of the Graduation Ball had evaporated and Arthur had spent his savings on an engagement ring for Mary (gold with a single diamond), they applied themselves to the pressing matter of jobs. They had decided not to marry for another year but could not bear the thought of living apart. Mary, whose plan for a swift return to Florence was put on hold, wanted to work in historical building conservation and had already submitted two applications: one, which sounded the more interesting, was to become Assistant Manager at a large National Trust property in Wiltshire; the other was to join the planning department of Norwich City Council. The application to the National Trust was quickly rejected: 'We have received a large number of applications from more experienced candidates and on this occasion we are sorry …'; but a week later a letter arrived inviting her for interview at City Hall in Norwich.

Although Norwich was less than fifty miles away, the journey by public transport was long and unreliable, so Mary's father was enlisted to drive. Arthur went along too: he knew very little of the city and wanted to know where they might be living if the interview went well. To Mary's disappointment, the members of the panel were starchy and expressionless, and they showed no interest in the glories of Florence. They wanted only to challenge her on planning laws (of which she knew little) and to discuss the problem of Norwich's redundant churches. They would let her know in due course. She came out despondent: they seemed such grey and unimaginative people. Her mood lifted a little as, in the afternoon, the three of them explored the city: the bustling market with its gaily coloured stalls, the awe-inspiring cathedral and its cloisters, the fourteenth-century Strangers' Hall, the cobbled streets of Tombland, and the river with its string of neatly moored holiday craft. Mary was especially excited by the Maddermarket Theatre, an eighteenth-century chapel transformed into an Elizabethan-style playhouse and home to the amateur Norwich Players. It was just a pity the interview had gone so badly.

A few days later, as she had expected, Mary received a brown envelope with a Norwich postmark and for a time, delaying the inevitable bad news, she did not bother to open it. But either she must have impressed the panel more than she thought, or the other candidates must have fared worse. 'We were impressed by your interview and references and are delighted to …' She did not bother to read the rest. 'Arthur,' she yelled, 'Guess what! They've actually offered me the job!' The salary was not as much as she had expected and she hoped her immediate colleagues would be friendlier than the stony-faced men she'd encountered, but you have to start somewhere, don't you? And this somewhere was Norwich, and in September, and it was too good an opportunity to turn down.

With Mary's immediate future settled, it was left to Arthur to focus on his own career. Over the past few months he had become more and more certain he wanted to teach – and to show that schools could be different from Sparrowhawk and Burgoyne – but he had no stomach for another year's study for a teaching qualification and he had left it late to find a position for the coming term. Enquiries, enclosing a carefully crafted cv, to almost every school in and around Norwich were predictably rebuffed: all posts had already been filled. But just as he began the search for some temporary work to tide him over, he had an unexpected approach from Thorpe Lodge, a small day preparatory school at Thorpe St Andrew on the southern outskirts of the city. A long-standing member of staff had fallen ill and there was, after all, a vacancy for a teacher of 'general subjects' (Dogsbody, thought Arthur). Was he by any chance still available? He was; and although it is difficult to tell much about a school when it is closed for the holidays and the classrooms are empty, a hastily arranged meeting with the jovial headmaster, Mr Williamson, convinced him that Thorpe Lodge was a happy place. There were girls as well as boys, tables instead of desks, white boards instead of black, and none of the throwbacks to Dotheboys Hall and the long-lost British Empire that had so bedevilled Sparrowhawk and Burgoyne. And since by now it was mid-August, and neither Mr Williamson nor Arthur had another option, they came to a rather loose agreement which would tide them both over until Christmas.

It only remained for Arthur and Mary to find somewhere to live, although that turned out to be harder than they had expected. Arthur's *Story* reads, 'For a time, it looked as if we would be homeless in Norwich, so we decided to renovate a run-down houseboat and we lived aboard for more than three years', but such a matter-of fact sentence tells nothing of their unlikely adventure. They had found the houseboat by chance. Or was it serendipity? Their quest for an affordable flat had taken them to agent after agent and they had drawn a blank. Everything in their price range had been snapped up by students from Norwich's own new and rapidly expanding university, so they had, for the moment, given up and Arthur had taken Mary to see where he would be working. Thorpe Lodge was a large but rather cosy-looking Georgian house which hid a plethora of temporary buildings behind, and the grounds were just large enough to squeeze in a playing field and a court for tennis and netball. 'It looks fabulous, Arthur,' said Mary. 'You're going to love it!' Arthur remained silent. He was suddenly unsure about the whole prospect. 'You'll be fine,' said Mary, reading his mind. 'I wish I'd had you as a teacher.'

Afterwards they had walked down to the River Yare and watched the hurrying boats. They had strolled across the bridge onto Thorpe Island where most of the hire craft were based. E.J. Warnes' Boatyard was almost empty, waiting for Saturday when its ten hire cruisers would disgorge their crews in the morning and be made ready for the next hoard of eager holidaymakers in the afternoon. But *Still Waters*, more like an oversized shoebox than a boat, lay there apart, unused and unloved. It started as a throwaway joke. 'I suppose we could live there, Arthur!' But perhaps ... perhaps it wasn't a joke after all.

In the office, Mr Warnes raised his bushy eyebrows. He had a friendly, weather-beaten, stubbly face and wore a cloth cap and a torn navy-blue jacket. On Saturday, when the new customers arrived, he would try to smarten himself up. He spoke with the unmistakable Norfolk burr. No, sadly there wasn't a demand for *Still Waters* anymore and he hadn't bothered to advertise her for some time. People wanted far more luxury these days and she simply wasn't worth spending money on. It was a shame, but at the end of the season she'd most likely be sold off or broken up. 'Well, yes, I suppose I might consider some sort of let until the end of the year, but it would be for you to smarten her up. With all the cruisers to maintain, I just don't have the staff. You're welcome to take the key and have a look, but I doubt she'll be any use to you. I'm afraid she's been dreadfully neglected.' In the corner, Nelson, a fierce-looking German Shepherd dog, yawned. Or more likely he was laughing.

Arthur and Mary took the key, though not without trepidation. *Still Waters* was a little over thirty feet long and about nine feet wide. The hull was black, the cream paint of the cabin was no longer cream, and varnish was peeling from the window frames. She did not look at all promising, but there could be no harm in going aboard. They stepped gingerly onto the small rectangular deck at the front ('The bow,' said Mary) and could feel the boat tilt slightly under their weight. There was enough room for sitting outside and maybe they could see themselves relaxing here with a glass of wine when the sun was over the yard-arm. But it took a superhuman stretch of the imagination and they had to tread carefully on the slippery green algae. They were mad even to think of it.

They unlocked the double doors that opened into the sparsely furnished cabin. On one side was a sofa bed; on the other were a small table and two chairs that had seen much better days. The once-bright gingham curtains were black with mildew and the carpet was stained and worn, but light poured invitingly through the four large windows. The living area led into a compact galley-kitchen, equipped with a fridge and a Calor Gas cooker. Neither had been cleaned since the last hirers had left two years before and one of the cupboard doors was hanging off. Opposite the galley was a cramped W.C. and shower compartment ('Yuk! Not very hygienic,' sniffed Mary), and beyond, built-in, were a double bunk ('Gross,' said Arthur, staring at the sagging, mouldering mattress), a large wardrobe and two chests of drawers. What could be better, though, than lying in bed and watching the comings and goings on the river?

Arthur and Mary looked at each other. Surely not, thought Arthur. 'It could be perfect,' said Mary who, in her mind's eye, was already seeing it transformed.

'There's a huge amount of work to do – and less than a month before we'd have to move in,' said Arthur.

'I know,' said Mary, 'but, come off it, Arthur, we've nowhere else to live, have we?' Which he had to admit was true. 'And it's close to Thorpe Lodge and on the bus route into the city. Or I could cycle and get fit.'

They examined everything more closely. The boat was damp from condensation, but there was no sign of any leaks in the roof. They assumed the water and electricity just had to be switched on. Mary's face was lit up with excitement. She was pacing out measurements and sketching a floor plan. 'It will be such an adventure, Arthur!' It was as if she were a character in some children's story. Outside the wavelets sparkled.

Arthur noticed how she said 'will', not 'could' or 'would'. 'I don't know. We have no idea how much it would cost us. Probably a fortune. There'd be the rent and all the materials we'd need. And …'

'Well, there's only one way to find out, isn't there?' Mary was not going to be put off that easily. 'Come on, let's at least ask Mr Warnes,' and, grasping Arthur purposefully by the hand, she led him back to the office.

'Come in and sit you down,' said Mr Warnes glumly. 'Not up to much, is she? I doubt she's what you're looking for.'

'We don't really know,' said Mary, trying to hide her enthusiasm. 'There's an awful lot more to do than we thought. It would all depend on the rent.'

Mr Warnes looked up. 'Are you trying to strike a bargain, young lady? To be honest, I'm surprised you've even given her a second look. Do you mean you might be interested in her?'

Mary gave him one of her smiles. 'As I said, Mr Warnes, it all depends. You see, we've only just finished university and we don't start work until next month. So we couldn't afford very much.'

Arthur looked on, helpless. He admired Mary's cheek, but he recognised that determined streak and he knew where it was leading.

Mr Warnes looked at them ruefully. 'Do you know, she's the first boat we built when I started working with my father, and that was just after the war when people didn't have much money? … It'd be right good if there was still some use for her. But times have moved on.'

'But does it leak?' asked Arthur, who was not going to be carried away by what was fast becoming an unlikely alliance.

'She, not it,' said Mary.

'Sound as a bell,' declared Mr Warnes. There was more than a hint of pride in his voice. Her hull's a steel pontoon and we used to take her out of the water every two years to black her. The cabin's built with a double skin so she's cosy in winter. It's just I've taken my eye off her.' He looked genuinely sad, as if she were his daughter and he had left her abandoned on the streets. 'Let me get us a cuppa …'

Mr Warnes turned out to be even more buoyed up than Mary at the prospect of bringing *Still Waters* back to life. He brought the tea. He offered them biscuits from a battered Tupperware container, then offered one to Nelson as well. Nelson drooled into the container as he chose. 'You'd have to do all the work yourselves, mind you, and there'd be some sort of rent if you managed to do her up.' They talked on. 'I tell you what,' he said. 'There's been a last-minute cancellation on one of our cruisers and she'll be lying idle for the next couple of weeks. If you're serious, you can sleep aboard her while you get *Still Waters* tidied up. Nelson lives in the boatshed. He'll look after you. I can't say fairer than that.' Nelson wagged his tail.

And so, almost without any of them noticing, it was agreed, although no one was quite sure what the deal was, and it didn't seem to matter. Mary stood up. 'I'm afraid we must rush off and catch our train, Mr Warnes. We've got to get back to Hunstanton tonight.'

'Is that where you're to?'

'I'm afraid so. It's a dreadful journey.'

'Well, let me drive you to the station. You've quite cheered me up. Who'd have thought …?'

'Who'd have thought?' echoed Arthur silently.

'We'll be back at the weekend to make a start,' said Mary. 'You have our word.'

They caught the train with a few minutes to spare. 'Are you sure we're doing the right thing?' said Arthur. 'There's just so much to do.'

'It'll be fine, Arthur. And if it doesn't work out, well, we won't have lost anything. Except a roof over our heads.'

'So what are you going to tell your parents? They'll be horrified.'

'Nothing, of course, until we've got her straight. But Mum will love her, I guarantee.'

Arthur was quiet. Mary sat making lists, began asking questions, drawing Arthur in until he, too, supposed it might be possible to make the boat half-habitable until they could find somewhere better.

'Habitable, Arthur? She'll be lovely – our first proper home.'

*

On Saturday they persuaded a friend to drive them to the boatyard. They had packed up all their belongings and it was a squeeze to fit everything into the car. There was nobody around at the University during the vacation to say goodbye, but it was a wrench nonetheless. They were leaving an important part of their life behind and, although they both had jobs to go to, where they would live was still as much a hope as a reality. They were excited (mainly Mary) and apprehensive (mainly Arthur). At the boatyard, it was turn-round day and an army of cleaners was preparing the hire boats for their next customers. A more presentable Mr Warnes greeted them like long-lost friends and took them across to the impressive motor cruiser which would be their temporary home: like a luxury cruise ship compared to *Still Waters*. He also showed them the boatshed, where he had cleared a corner for them to store anything bulky and all the things they would have to buy for *Still Waters*. 'I'll leave you to get settled in, but don't hesitate to ask if you need anything. Oh, and help yourself to any of the cleaning stuff in that cupboard over there.' Nelson bounded over and waited for his grubby ball to be thrown.

Arthur and Mary changed into their oldest clothes. It was only early afternoon and there was time to make a start on the cleaning. On *Still Waters* they saw the deck had been pressure-washed and now had a welcoming glow: Mr Warnes was going to be an ally. In the cabin, however, even Mary was struck by the enormity of the task ahead of them. They had decided to tackle the inside first and worry about the outside afterwards. First, they took the mattress, the carpet, the curtains, and the battle-scarred kitchen worktop to the skip, and stored the salvageable furniture in the boatshed. Then Arthur scrubbed the living area from top to bottom, while Mary attacked the galley. At the end of the afternoon, once he had waved off the last of the hire boats, Mr Warnes came over to see how they were getting on. 'My, it's a grand job you're doing. I take my hat off to you!' He raised his ageing cap. 'Come next week, you'll be ready to start some painting.'

'She's coming on, isn't she?' said Mary. Even Arthur's doubts were beginning to fade. 'And thank you ever so much for doing the deck for us. It looks beautiful.'

Mr Warnes looked round. 'You've had a real good clear-out, haven't you? Now don't you go buying any new stuff without asking me. There are plenty of odds and ends lying around I'd be glad to get rid of.'

Arthur and Mary felt they'd done more than enough for one day. Before the boatshed was locked for the weekend, Mary collected some mould remover and disinfectant which she'd need for cleaning the shower. They made tea and ate chunks of the cake Mary had baked. Once they had washed off the dirt and dust and smartened themselves up, they headed off to stock up with provisions, but this evening they would treat themselves to a meal in the local hostelry. That night they lay awake, listening to the lap-lapping of the water on the hull. They realised they had never slept on a boat before, but this is how it could be for the foreseeable future.

On Sunday, they did the rest of the cleaning. On Monday, they sandpapered all the paintwork – a job they hated – and borrowed a vacuum cleaner to hoover up the dust. On Tuesday, Mr Warnes, accompanied by Nelson, showed them to a shelf of half-used cans of paint. 'Take your pick. You'll need at least two coats, mind you. And there's some varnish over there for the window frames. There are plenty of brushes as long as you look after them.' They chose a sandy beige for the walls and a muted red for the wardrobe and drawers, and the cupboards in the galley, and spent the following days painting. All the time they worked tirelessly, taking pleasure in their joint enterprise. They laughed and joked; sometimes argued fiercely over a point of detail; spoke seriously about the past and the future; sang along to the radio; shared their dreams and their fears; found out more about each other than the demands of university life had allowed; and (fortunately) they liked what they found.

On Thursday, while they were waiting for a second coat of paint to dry, they caught the bus into Norwich. In a dingy house-clearance shop in Magdalen Street, they found a tall bookcase they thought would just fit in, an oil-filled electric radiator for the winter, and a couple of antiquarian prints of the Norfolk rivers which would look good alongside Mary's own artwork on the cabin walls – the shopkeeper would drop them all off when he was out that way. On the market, Mary found some material with a cheerful nautical pattern that would be ideal for the curtains. 'We are sure about this boat, aren't we?' asked Mary mischievously. By now, Arthur's misgivings had evaporated. They were both more than sure.

Mr Warnes visited them every day, usually twice, to admire their handiwork and to point out, not very subtly, where they might be able to improve. On Friday, taking him at his word, Arthur asked about the remaining things they needed. Yes, there were some offcuts of worktops in the boatshed and they could help themselves. One of the workmen would do the cutting for them. No, he didn't have any spare carpet or vinyl, but there was a shop on the Sprowston Road that always had cheap roll-ends. But, yes, he had a perfectly good mattress that wouldn't fit the bunks in the new cruisers; he couldn't give it to them, but he'd work out a decent price. Mary bought petunias and geraniums, which someone in the village was selling from their garden, planted them in two washing-up bowls salvaged from the skip and placed them on the roof. At the weekend, they put on the final coats of paint and admired their glistening handiwork.

The following week, Mary went home, both to break it to her parents where she and Arthur would be living – and, importantly, to use her mother's sewing machine to make the curtains. If they were still on speaking terms, she hoped they would drive her back to Norwich with some of the essentials saved from her bedsit the year before and, with luck, give *Still Waters* their seal of approval. While she was away, Arthur spent a day replacing the kitchen worktop and with two other offcuts making a desk for each of them – for Mary in the bedroom and for himself in the living area. It was slow work, but he was surprised at how much he had learned helping Grandpa in his workshop, and he found pleasure and satisfaction when working with his hands. The cuts and scratches were a small price to pay. The next day he fitted the carpet and vinyl they had managed to buy: he made mistakes, but ones that only he would notice. On the morning Mary was due to return with her parents, he cleaned the furniture they had stored in the boatshed and, with the help of Mr Warnes' son, Jack, carried it back and put it in place. There was just enough time for him to wipe down the side of the boat which faced the car park so it would not look quite so dilapidated to their visitors. He crossed his fingers and hoped they would approve. He ought to tell Grandpa and Grandma what they were up to, but he'd wait until he had some photographs to show them.

The inspection party arrived. Mary's mother could not wait to go aboard. 'But it's wonderful,' she said. 'You've done it brilliantly.' Arthur could see how Mary's optimism and smile had been inherited from her mother. Mary's father, a cautious accountant, felt the joints of Arthur's woodwork, ran his hand over the paintwork, and nodded approvingly. He asked about the electricity and water, and how *Still Waters* had been built. 'I confess I was pretty worried when Mary told us what you were doing, but you've made a good job of it.' Mary could not remember his ever being so effusive. Mr Warnes came over. 'Lovely job, isn't it? You ought to be very proud of them.'

'We are,' said Mary's mother. 'And we gather you've helped them all the way and been so generous, too. Thank you for everything you've done for them.'

'It's been a pleasure, ma'am. I never thought I'd see the old boat come back to life. Heading for the scrapyard, she was. They can stay here as long as they like, and I hope they will.'

Mary's father collected two folding director's chairs from the car and he and Arthur sat out on the deck talking of this and that, and especially of Arthur's job at Thorpe Lodge. Mary and her mother set about putting up the curtains. There was lunch at the pub and in the afternoon they unloaded the car of all the things Mary and her mother had collected together – bed linen and towels, crockery and cutlery, pots and pans, clothes and more clothes, shoes and more shoes, and all the stuff that is too often forgotten. 'Enough to sink a battleship!' said Mary's father, and that was before they moved in the belongings that Arthur and Mary had brought from university and were still stacked in the shed. They switched on the Calor Gas, Mary made tea, and they tucked into the scones and flapjacks brought from home. 'It's like playing doll's houses, isn't it?' she said. Then there were a bottle of whisky for Mr Warnes, a hug, a kiss, and a wave, and both Mary and her mother shed a tear, and at last Arthur and Mary were on their own. Tomorrow they would clean down the rest of *Still Waters*' exterior – painting it would have to wait – but now they opened a bottle of wine and sat outside watching the ducks, the coots and the moorhens paddling idly by, and were still there, exhausted and elated, when the sky turned red. That night was the first they slept on *Still Waters*. She rocked gently beneath them.

*

Alice studies the photograph of *Still Waters*. In his own way, and not with any consistency, Arthur has told her many times about their life afloat. 'You loved that boat, didn't you Arthur?'

'Yes,' says Arthur. 'We'd never done ... anything like it before. ... It wasn't always easy ... but we did it ... together. ... It was very special living ... on the water. ... A bit bouncy sometimes. ... Boats going too fast. ... Mr Warnes was very good to us. We helped him look after ... the boatyard ... and he ... looked after us. ... I don't think he ever ... charged us any rent.'

After a while, Arthur turns the page and reads haltingly. 'I married Mary on 15 July 1967. ... The wedding was at St Andrew's Church at Thorpe ... which overlooks the Green and the River. As a wedding present ... Mr Warnes lent us one of his hire cruisers ... for a week. ... After the reception we walked down to the river ... and climbed aboard and ... everyone waved us off on our honeymoon.' He looks at the photographs. There are two of them on the page. The first is a formal photograph taken outside the church. All top hats, tails and summer frocks. Alice points at each of them in turn.

'They're your grandpa and grandma, aren't they, Arthur?'

'Yes, that's right.'

'And who are they?'

'They must be ... Mary's mother and father.'

'And him?'

'That's ... Ray. Mary met him in Florence. He was a good friend.'

'Was he your best man?'

Arthur pauses. Then, slowly, 'Yes ... I believe he was.'

'And who are those sweet little bridesmaids?'

'I think they were ... from Mary's family.'

The second photograph captures Arthur carrying Mary aboard. They are so happy. 'It's lucky you didn't drop Mary in!' says Alice 'But what a glorious way to spend your honeymoon? Where did you go?'

'All over the Broads. From Beccles in the south to ... Stalham ... in the north. Sometimes we moored up outside a pub ... and sometimes we dropped the mud weight … in the middle of a Broad … so we were quite … alone.'

Of course, Alice knows all these answers and, on the days when Arthur cannot quite remember, she is able to help him.

'Are you … married, Alice?' It is the question Arthur always asks and always catches her off guard. Her tears well up.

'No, Arthur. I was going to get married last summer, but it never happened.'

It was, in fact, only a few weeks before the planned wedding that Alice's fiancé was killed. A car hit his motorcycle and he was dead before the paramedics arrived. For months Alice was consumed by grief. To an extent, she still is, but it is the job at Marsh View that has helped to save her. She has channelled her love into the residents and they have loved her in return. 'Oh dear,' says Arthur. 'I'm sure you will … get married one day.'

'We'll see,' says Alice, surreptitiously wiping her eyes, and she turns the page.

'Are you … married, Alice?' asks Arthur.

*

As it turned out, Arthur and Mary spent more than three years living on *Still Waters*. They became unofficial caretakers of the boatyard and when things were especially busy they would lend a hand with the hire boats. In marked contrast to the dreary atmosphere of her interview, Mary was relieved to find the office at City Hall a lively place. She enjoyed her job and, as might have been predicted, it was not long before she was promoted. To begin with, Arthur found life at Thorpe Lodge a challenge and he wasn't sure he was cut out to be a teacher after all. Planning lessons, marking books and making workcards took far more time than he had expected; outside the classroom, there were activities to supervise and duties to be done; and, until he became used to them, he worried unnecessarily about staff meetings, parents' evenings and open days – occasions when he felt callow and inadequate.

However, Arthur's colleagues were supportive without being too intrusive; more importantly, he liked the children and they liked him. 'He's a bright spark,' said a nine-year-old wit, so 'Sparky' he became for ever, although he was not really sparky at all. He was firm but fair, friendly but not too friendly, empathetic and approachable, and little by little he grew in confidence. After a few weeks, his classes became orderly and respectful. Instead of the extremes of noise, anger and silence, they settled into the low buzz of work. Mr Williamson sat in on some of Arthur's lessons and was impressed. Arthur was well prepared, his marking was thorough but encouraging, and there were eye-catching displays of children's work on his classroom walls (Mary, with her artistic flair, had more than a hand in these).

'You're a natural, Arthur,' said Mr Williamson at the end of the first half term. 'Sadly, Mr Potts won't be coming back, so I rather hope you'll consider staying with us permanently – if you haven't anything else fixed up.'

Arthur was relieved. All the time he'd been wondering if he was good enough and he was. 'That's very generous of you, Headmaster,' he said, not quite overcome with emotion. 'I did have some doubts at first, but I'm beginning to get the hang of it.' And, yes, if it was all right, he would very much like to stay on.

So Arthur settled into the rhythm of the school year: the carol service at Christmas, the school play at Easter, exams in the summer – and sports day, when the mothers wore hats; the competitive fathers coached; the children cheered; Mr Williamson presented the silver cups and made a speech; and afterwards there were tea and cake, and strawberries and cream, for everyone.

*

But although on the surface everything was serene, disturbing undercurrents were swirling beneath. During the school holidays, while Mary was still at work, Arthur would spend time with Grandpa and Grandma, and he noticed how they were beginning to look old. They were in their eighties, after all. Grandpa was gaunt and ashen. He often seemed breathless, and Grandma fussed over him and was becoming tired herself. They were too proud to say anything to him and, when his tactful questions were rebuffed, there was not much he could do to help – except to telephone and visit them more often. On one visit, by chance, he met Norman again. They went out for a drink and reminisced about their childhood days: two young boys who had taken different paths, grown up, become teacher and architect, and were once more comfortable in each other's company. 'You live on a houseboat?' asked Norman incredulously. 'It must be hideously cramped. Aren't you seasick?'

'No, it's fine. We love it on the river. You must come and stay sometime and see for yourself.'

'I might just take you up on that.'

On another visit Arthur met Sarah in the village shop. For a moment he was taken aback. It was an age since their childhood escapade, but he could feel himself blushing. 'Sarah, what are you doing here? I thought you were still living down south.' It turned out to be a long story, told in salacious detail in the aisle between the bread and the biscuits.

Sarah told him how she had hated life at her girls' school. She had been suspended a couple of times but had just about survived. She had scraped enough A levels to study sociology at the glitzy University of Watermouth on the south coast, where she had been one of the stream of students seduced by the notorious Howard Kirk, the 'History Man' (No surprise there, thought Arthur) and, probably as a result, had gained a remarkably good degree. While she had been away, her father had had an affair with his new secretary and had moved out to live with her. There had been an acrimonious divorce.

After university, Sarah had returned home to live with her mother, but she hadn't been able to find a meaningful job ('I mean, Arthur, what use is a sociology degree to anyone? I only did it because the numpty careers teacher told me it was a waste of time. And what did she know? Stuck up cow'). She had worked in a bar and been swept off her feet by a married Casanova (No surprise there either, thought Arthur, except she probably did the sweeping). When that ended in inevitable tears, she had retreated to Hartbourne, taking refuge with her Aunt Dorothy, and was now working as an estate agent in Grantham.

'Let me know next time you're here and we'll have a meal together,' said Sarah.

Arthur smelled danger. 'Don't forget, I'm a happily married man.'

'I like married men,' said Sarah.

Later that year, Norman did take Arthur up on his offer and came to stay on *Still Waters*. The three of them dined on board and the flickering candles cast dancing shadows around the tiny cabin. He wouldn't want to live on a boat himself – it would be too claustrophobic – but he could see the attraction. Arthur was pleased their schoolboy friendship had been re-established and, as the shadows danced, Mary felt a connection with the good-looking and quietly confident architect who understood about planning and building, and she was captivated by his infectious grin. The sofa bed wasn't that uncomfortable, and Norman, who was equally smitten by Mary, became a frequent visitor. Another visitor was Ray, who arrived in a stylish Italian suit and a new sports car – a Lamborghini. He waxed more than lyrical about *Still Waters* – 'Isn't she just cute?' – but (he said tactfully) he did not want to intrude on their space and booked himself into Norwich's more salubrious Royal Hotel where he entertained them sumptuously. They did not feel at all insulted.

*

This morning it is Matron who comes in to wake Arthur. She puts a mug of tea beside his bed, then breezily sweeps back the curtains. 'It's another nice day, Arthur. Will you have breakfast in the dining room or in here?'

'In here, I think,' says Arthur. It is almost always in here. He can do without the dining room with the endless clatter of plates and 'What would you like today, darling?' He has forgotten his first disastrous lunchtime at Marsh View, but he dislikes all the old people and their repetitive questions. He feels rather sorry for them. Please don't let me be like that.

'Would you like the radio on?'

Arthur likes the radio. At least, he likes listening to music – not heavily classical, but folk, country, songs from the shows. Proper songs from the 1960s and 70s. He cannot follow talk programmes anymore and has given up on television. It is all too confusing. Matron puts on Radio 2. By chance they are playing Leonard Cohen – 'Suzanne takes you down to her place near the river ...' – and somehow it makes a connection. *Still Waters* floats into his mind. 'You can hear the boats go by, you can spend the night beside her ...' 'I think Mary ... is coming today,' he says.

'That'll be nice,' says Matron, but she knows Mary will not come.

'We lived ... on a boat once.'

'Did you? I like boats.' She picks up an empty water glass. 'Joan will be along soon to help you get dressed.'

Arthur does not like Joan very much. She is loud and is always in a hurry. 'Is Mary ... coming today?' he asks.

*

To begin with, Arthur and Mary revelled in their life on the river, but after a time and notwithstanding the apparent freedom *Still Waters* offered, they fell into a dull routine and began to feel their horizons were closing in. Afloat, they no longer kissed each other goodbye as they set off for work, and in the evenings Arthur sat at his desk marking books while Mary mulled over plans, read or sewed. They were still in love and there was no rift between them, but too often in their busy lives they were taking each other for granted. Sometimes Arthur would think of Sarah: life with her would have been a rollercoaster – not one he would have wanted, but he couldn't help admiring her devil-may-care approach. And sometimes Mary's mind would wander. She would see herself lying with Norman on a secluded, sun-drenched beach, and would look forward eagerly to his next visit (she wasn't sure if it was the sun-drenched beach or Norman which attracted her more). Ashore, Arthur and Mary slipped into their own separate niches at the Maddermarket – Mary on stage and Arthur, more reluctantly, behind the scenes; although neither considered themselves religious, they found the occasional service at the Cathedral uplifting; and they never tired of the noisy busyness of the market; but more and more they wanted to escape the confines of *Still Waters*' cabin and of their working lives. They missed the marshes and the sea, and even visits to Grandpa and Grandma, and to Mary's parents, which entailed tiresome journeys on public transport, had become just another part of the routine. On top of that, Mary often longed for the carefree days in Florence. 'I love it here, Arthur,' 'but it's all so cramped. We need to get out more and get away. We've got so boring. We need to get some excitement back in our lives.'

Arthur did not disagree. They had both learned to drive before going to university and, now they were earning, they could afford a car. In the summer of 1968, they bought an elderly dark-blue Sunbeam with red leather seats and no synchromesh on second gear. It was Arthur's pride and joy. At weekends they returned to their old haunts on the north coast and explored some of the great houses; family visits were no longer such a chore; and they were able to go on holiday further afield. They indulged in the comparative luxury of second-rate hotels ('We spend the rest of our lives sort of camping,' said Mary, 'so let's just splash out once in a while.'). Arthur took them to castles and battlefields, and had a habit of diving into museums and old churches; Mary humoured him, but preferred diving into the sea and walking in the hills – the Peak District, Snowdonia, the Pennine Way: she told him he was developing a paunch and needed to take more exercise. Then, when it was approaching their second wedding anniversary, 'Let's have another honeymoon,' said Mary. 'I'm going to take you to Florence at last.' She wrote to her old landlady – 'Yes, of course you can stay with us' – and booked the flights for the third week in July. 'You're going to adore it, Arthur. I know it,' and she was happy again.

And Arthur did adore it. He adored seeing the cathedrals and the galleries Mary had told him so much about. He adored meeting the shopkeepers and the families who ran the hidden trattorias Mary had frequented. They all remembered her – how could they not? – and kissed her on both cheeks, and nothing was too much trouble. He adored strolling along the bank of the Arno and, because he was with Mary, he thought himself a local like her and not one of the crowd of camera-clicking tourists. He adored seeing her smile as she used to smile, and knew why he had married her, and fell in love all over again. *Still Waters* had in so many ways been an idyll, but in Florence he saw how it would soon be time to move on. They would save up for a deposit, buy a house, start a family, but not yet become too much a part of the bourgeoisie. After they had made love, trying hard not to make the bed squeak, he told all this to Mary, who had been thinking exactly the same. They poured a glass of Prosecco, which they had put conveniently on the bedside table, drank a toast 'To Us and to the Future!' and, as they do in the films, fell asleep in each other's arms.

*

At Marsh View, 'Is Mary … coming today?' asks Arthur anxiously. A grey mist is blowing in from the sea.

IV

Ashore

Perhaps Arthur failed to see the trap, but how could he not? Or perhaps he did see it but considered himself wary enough not to be caught. Once bitten ... Or perhaps (although he would never admit it) it was the trap itself that excited him and he half wanted to be caught, and he knew exactly what was going to happen.

It was an evening in early September, not long after the sojourn in Florence and as the long school holiday was drawing to a close. Arthur had made his by now regular journey in the Sunbeam to see Grandpa and Grandma and was staying with them for a few days while Mary was working on her empty churches. There were jobs in the garden that Grandpa was no longer capable of doing and anyway they just liked having him for company. It all began when he met Sarah again as he walked along to the shop for a few things Grandma had forgotten.

'Back already, Arthur? You're becoming quite a regular. I hope your grandpa's getting on all right.'

Arthur
looked dubious. 'He's not too good, I'm afraid, but he struggles on and he never complains. It's a depressing business, getting old. He doesn't get out much now, but at least his mind's as sharp as ever, which is a blessing. Better that than not knowing who or where you are.'

'Not nice, though, is it? Why don't you come round for that meal, Arthur? It'd cheer you up. Aunt Dorothy's away with her sister at the moment, so I've got the house to myself. I'll ask Norman to join us if he's around. I know he'd like to catch up with you as well. Let's do it tomorrow, if you're still here?'

There was a moment's hesitation. Then, 'That'd be good, Sarah. I'll check with Grandpa and Grandma, but I'm sure they won't mind.'

'Eight o'clock be all right? It'd give me time to rustle up something after work. I'm afraid it'll be very casual.'

'Casual's fine. I've only got gardening clothes with me. So, yes, eight tomorrow would be great, unless I call you later. Thanks a lot, Sarah. I'll look forward to it.'

'Me too. See you then.' She blew him a provocative kiss.

*

Aunt Dorothy's house was at the other end of the village and the next evening, at eight o'clock, Arthur knocked on the door. After a few seconds, Sarah opened it. 'Arthur, come in, come in. Lovely to see you.' She gave him a hug, which sent a frisson of desire through his body. As he had expected, she looked stunning. She was wearing a low-cut turquoise dress, with matching earrings and pendant, and he remembered the turquoise tee shirt she had worn when they went to Grantham together. He handed her a bottle of wine. 'All the shop could manage, I'm afraid.'

Sarah showed him into the living room, which had an old person's furniture and pictures. But Sarah had cheered it up with candles burning in the hearth and at the far end the table had a bright red cloth and another candle burning in its centre. Arthur noticed it was only set for two and it did not look casual at all.

'Let me pour you a drink,' said Sarah. 'Shall we start on the wine, or I'm sure I can find something else in the sideboard? Aunt Dot's bound to have some Bristol Cream stashed away.'

Arthur pulled a face. 'Wine's fine.'

'I'm afraid Norman can't make it,' said Sarah, as she found some glasses. 'Something on at work, apparently. So it's just us.'

'That's a shame. I was looking forward to seeing him.' Of course he couldn't come, thought Arthur. I bet she never asked him. He wasn't sure if it were a shame or not.

They drank wine. Sarah told him more about her failed romance, but she didn't seem too cut up about it. Win some, lose some: it was another of life's adventures. It was this sort of happy-go-lucky attitude that captivated Arthur. It was so different from the steady life he and Mary enjoyed on *Still Waters*. He could not stop glancing at Sarah's revealing dress and she knew it; and he could not help imagining her without the dress, just as she had been in the woodland clearing all those years ago. 'Gather ye rosebuds while ye may, Arthur,' said Sarah. 'You'll be like your grandpa before you know it.'

She was right, thought Arthur. After all, it was what he and Mary had been feeling. In Florence they had broken free from their staleness, but already, partly because of Grandpa's health, they had begun to slip back into their old routine. Soon he would be starting another term at Thorpe Lodge – a new academic year, but nothing would change apart from the children's names.

Sarah poured more wine. 'Bring it into the kitchen, so we can carry on while I fix some supper.' She put a lasagne, which she had already prepared, into the oven and mixed up a salad. Then she produced two prawn cocktails. 'Two I made earlier! Let's take them through and have them while the lasagne heats up.' And, looking at their empty glasses, 'Oh, and I'd better open another bottle. Shall we have the one you brought?'

As they ate, Arthur talked about how he'd met Mary at university, and the plays they'd worked on together, and how they'd found *Still Waters* and turned her into a floating home. He told her how miserable he'd been at Burgoyne, where bullying had been an accepted part of the culture, and how he and Mary were happy but life was no longer an adventure (I don't know why I'm telling her this, he thought). The trip to Florence had helped – she ought to go sometime, she'd love it – but there was still something missing. Sarah recounted the misery of her family falling apart. She couldn't forgive her father, and his mistress was a shameless flirt (Pot, kettle, black, thought Arthur), but she supposed her mother wasn't without blame. She wasn't enjoying being an estate agent. It was all so frantic. There were targets to be met, so she was having to sell people houses they didn't want. Anyway, she couldn't stay with Aunt Dorothy for ever and she'd decided to move back to Watermouth. It was a lively place, even if a bit run-down, and she knew people there and she missed living by the sea. When Arthur next visited, she'd probably have gone. 'But this time I will keep in touch. Promise.' Although he didn't say so, Arthur wasn't sure that would be a good idea. It was all rather maudlin. They finished the second bottle of wine. One of the candles guttered and died.

Sarah made coffee. They sat together on the sofa. She really is incredibly alluring, thought Arthur. But she's flighty and irresponsible, everything that Mary isn't, and not in a good way. It had been a great evening, but he ought to be going. 'Please, not yet,' said Sarah. She rested her head on his shoulder, kissed him, lightly at first, then fiercely, laid her hand on his thigh, edged it upwards. Arthur saw where this was heading, knew he had to go before the trap snapped shut, did not move, let the wine cloud his judgement. Sarah stood up, took his hand. 'Come on, Arthur, for old times' sake,' and she led him towards the stairs.

It was almost midnight when Arthur left and the chill air had a sobering effect. The sky was clear and there was a nearly full moon, an amber warning. 'Ill met by moonlight', he thought. No one was about and only the odd light glimmered from the houses down the street, but he could sense people watching from behind their twitching curtains. He passed Mrs Jones' house. She was old now, but she would guess where he had been, just as she had surely guessed all those years ago, and he blushed, as he had done then, in the darkness. Quietly he let himself in, treading carefully so as not to disturb Grandpa and Grandma. For a long time he remained awake, agonising over how he could have been so stupid, although he had always feared and hoped how the evening would end. The morning brought him a headache but no comfort. He showered vigorously, but still he felt unclean. He couldn't go back to Mary with Sarah's heady perfume lingering on him. Later, as he was about to leave for home, Grandpa said, 'I heard you creeping in last night, Arthur. It's none of my business what you get up to with Sarah, and I don't want to know, but you're a married man and you couldn't have chosen a better wife than Mary. I just hope you're not doing anything to hurt her.'

Arthur nodded. Grandpa was right, it was none of his business, he thought angrily. Yet he was right about Mary, too. 'It's OK, Grandpa, you've no need to worry. I promise nothing happened.'

*

While Arthur was driving, the events at Aunt Dorothy's turned over and over in his mind. He had enjoyed the warmth, the food and the wine. He had known what Sarah was like and from the outset he had known things might be heading towards the bedroom. Although he had drunk too much, he could easily have picked up his coat and left, but he had chosen not to. There had been something thrilling about the subterfuge. Sarah had no inhibitions and the sex, let's face it, had been good: Sarah was an original and energetic instructor. He had only himself to blame. In a way, however, what happened had cleared his thinking. Sarah was moving away, and that was a relief. He had been weak and selfish, but soon she would no longer be there to tempt him. Mary was worth a hundred Sarahs. She was clever, and reliable, and in her own way just as beautiful, but recently he had too often taken her for granted and now, after everything they had said to each other in Florence, he had betrayed her. However, despite what they had always agreed, he was certain that for this once honesty would not be the best policy. What he had done was unforgiveable: if Mary found out, she would have every right to slap his face and throw him out. It would have to remain a secret, even if that meant it would keep coming back to haunt him. As long as he behaved naturally when he got back to Thorpe, he was sure Mary would not discover his aberration. He would, in his own way, make it up to her, but if it happened again. ... No, it would never happen again.

When Arthur arrived at the boatyard it was late afternoon and Nelson rushed over to greet him. Mary had got back from the office and was sitting on *Still Waters'* deck, reading.

'Hi, Arthur. You're just in time. I was about to make a cup of tea. Did you have a good journey?'

'Mm. Tea would be good, thank you. I'm parched. There wasn't much traffic today, so I didn't stop.' He bent down and kissed her cheek. 'Have you missed me then?'

'Of course. I always miss you.' Arthur's stomach churned. 'How are Grandpa and Grandma?'

'Much the same, I think. They send their love. Grandpa's pretty breathless, though. It might be nice if they came to stay here for a weekend while the weather's good. But I'd have to go and pick them up. I'm not sure Grandpa would be able to drive this far.'

Grandpa and Grandma did not, of course, stay on board when they came to visit. They liked their privacy and were certainly past sofa beds. But there was a small hotel in Thorpe near the Green. It was old-fashioned, but so were they, and it suited them.

'Yes, let's invite them. I'm sure they could do with a break, and they enjoy pottering around in Norwich.'

Arthur unfolded a second chair. Mary went below to make the tea and brought it out with a plate of cookies. 'A special treat, Arthur. I made them last night.' Arthur's stomach churned again.

They chatted on. Mary was enthusiastic about a new planning project and explained it in great detail. Arthur didn't really listen. He told her how he'd met his childhood friend Sarah again – about her move south when they'd still been at school, university at Watermouth, her parents' travails, her own disastrous love affair and return to Aunt Dorothy in Hartbourne. Now she was throwing in her estate agent's job and going back to Watermouth, where her heart seemed to be.

'I wonder what that'll be like,' wondered Mary, 'now she's not a student anymore and most of her friends have moved on. I reckon I'd feel a bit strange. Maybe it's different when it's a big town, and it would be great to live on the coast. But I bet it's rather dead in winter. I hope she's thought it through.'

'I shouldn't think so for a minute,' said Arthur. 'I don't reckon Sarah's ever thought things through and she seems to have caused chaos wherever she's been, but somehow she's managed to survive. I bet Aunt Dorothy will be grateful to have some peace and quiet.'

For a moment there was an uneasy silence. A boat went past and *Still Waters* rocked in its wash. 'I wish they'd slow down,' said Mary. Another silence. Arthur knew Mary too well. There was something she wanted to say and wasn't saying. She couldn't have guessed, could she? He didn't know how long he could keep this up. 'Shall we go for a drink this evening?' suggested Mary.

'Good idea. But what's this in aid of? I've only been away three days.'

'Away with your feckless friend Sarah,' said Mary accusingly.

Arthur reddened. How could she possibly know? It was only last night he'd been with Sarah. 'We didn't ...'

'Don't be silly, Arthur. I'm sure you didn't. I'm only teasing ... I hope.'

'Look, Mary, there's nothing between me and Sarah. Honestly. No way is she my type.'

Mary hesitated — or was it in Arthur's imagination? 'I'm sure there isn't. Come here.' She put her arm round him.

Nelson ambled over, the ball in his mouth, and looked at them expectantly.

*

'What will you have?' asked Arthur. They were sitting outside the pub, looking across the Green to the river. They were surrounded by boaters recounting the day's exploits — the swirling tides through Great Yarmouth; the expanse of Breydon Water that was more like being at sea; dodging the chain ferry at Reedham; navigating the twists and turns of the River Chet. Tales that grew taller with every pint.

'I'll have an orange juice, please,' said Mary.

'Orange juice? That's not like you. You've brought me here for an orange juice?' Then, more concerned, 'You're feeling all right, aren't you?'

'I'm fine, Arthur. I just fancy an orange juice.' Arthur went to buy the drinks and returned with Mary's juice, a pint of Adnams and a couple of packets of crisps. 'Thanks, Arthur. Cheers!' and they clinked glasses.

'So what did you get up to when you were away?' asked Mary. 'Apart from your fling with Sarah.'

'What's this obsession with Sarah?' said Arthur tetchily. 'I just met her again and she told me she was going back to Watermouth. I wish I hadn't told you about her. ... No, I mowed the lawn as usual and did a few things in the house. It's a shame, but the place is getting too much for them.'

Did Arthur's uncharacteristic edginess lead Mary to suspect something untoward had happened with Sarah? Not at the time: she loved and trusted him too much, and she was too excited by what she was about to tell him. But perhaps her teasing was also in part a warning – Don't spoil things for us, Arthur. There's too much at stake – and one day she would look back and wonder. For a while they sat in uneasy silence. Arthur looked up: Mary was gazing at her drink, the trace of that smile playing on her lips: she had never looked more beautiful and his heart missed a beat. It was a glorious evening, but inside he felt downhearted and ashamed. 'Come on, Mary. I know you've got something to tell me. I knew as soon as I got back.'

Mary looked up and the full radiant smile spread across her face. 'I've got some good news, Arthur. Or, we've got some good news.'

Arthur wasn't in the mood for good news, but he did his best to look interested. 'Go on,' he said.

'I'm expecting a baby. Sorry, we're expecting a baby.'

Arthur's heart missed another beat. It should have been one of the best moments in his life and already he had ruined it.

'Don't look so appalled,' said Mary. 'Aren't you pleased?'

'Of course I am. I'm more than pleased. I just wasn't expecting it, that's all. It wasn't in the plan quite yet. But hey …' He leant across and kissed her. 'I'd get a bottle of champagne, but I suppose you'd rather stick to orange juice?'

''Fraid so. That's the way it's going to be for a while.'

They talked on. Mary wanted to tell Arthur all about it and he wanted to hear it all. He only wished he hadn't messed things up so badly. It was something he would always regret, but he would have to try to put it behind him. The baby had, it seemed, been conceived in Florence, and where could have been better? Twice Mary had missed her period, felt a bit queasy in the mornings, and only that day had gone to the doctor who had confirmed what she already knew. No, we should wait a little longer before we tell Mum and Dad or anyone else – just to be certain everything's fine. 'Yes, of course it will be fine, Arthur, but you know what I mean. Let's at least wait until the end of the month.'

'A water baby,' murmured Mary that night as they cuddled up in bed. It began to rain, and the raindrops pattering noisily on the roof gave them a sense of security; but for all its magic – a magic that between them Arthur and Mary had helped to create – they knew that the cramped cabin of *Still Waters* was not the ideal place for a baby or even for a pregnant mother. Their life afloat was coming to an end.

*

As it turned out, by the time parents and grandparents were told, to great excitement, that Mary was expecting, it had been discovered there were not just one, but two little water babies on the way. Mary's mother was ecstatic; her father was quietly pleased. Grandma couldn't wait to start knitting and, most importantly from a practical point of view, Grandpa reminded Arthur that his mother had left some savings to him in trust until he reached the age of twenty-five. It had been at the back of Arthur's mind, but he had assumed it would be a tiny sum and had not yet bothered to explore it. In fact, it would be enough for the deposit on a small house and if necessary Grandpa would loan them the money until the inheritance was released.

Then they told Mr Warnes. He pretended to weep and dabbed his eyes with his greasy handkerchief, but he was delighted for them and understood they would want to move on. 'I'm going to miss you, and that's a fact. ... I never thought you'd last here for three months, let alone three years. ... My lad Jack'll be joining the yard next year and he'll be needing somewhere to live. That boat might be just the ticket. ... Now don't you go forgetting us. We'll want to see the babies, of course, and you know you'll always be welcome here. ... Quite part of the family. ... And who knows, there might even be a cruiser for you to take the babes on holiday next year.'

Property in Thorpe St Andrew was out of Arthur and Mary's price-range, but the terraced streets in Thorpe Hamlet, a little closer to the city centre, were more affordable, and something there would still allow Arthur to walk to work. They made a list of priorities.

Ideally three bedrooms; an upstairs bathroom if possible; a small, enclosed garden; an area that seemed quiet and cared for. They picked up property details and over two or three evenings took to exploring from the outside. It did not take them long to discover that an estate agent's camera is designed to be selective with the truth even if it does not lie, and houses which looked in need of major work, or which were in unkempt roads, or which had youths loitering nearby, were quickly rejected. They drew up a short list, dragged in Mary's parents to give a second opinion, and organised a drizzly weekend of viewings. Some houses, which had seemed promising from the particulars, needed too much renovation; others, which had been recently refurbished, they found soulless. It was only late on the Sunday afternoon, when the drizzle had turned into rain, that they came, huddled together, to the last house on their list, The Moorings. It was some distance from the river, so why it was called The Moorings was anyone's guess. 'Maybe it's a good omen,' said Mary, trying to keep everyone cheerful.

'Any port in a storm,' grumbled Arthur, as the rain poured down.

From the outside, The Moorings looked much like everywhere else they had been, but somehow it felt more inviting. The tiny front garden was neat and full of colour; the step was scrubbed; the doorknocker was newly polished. They were welcomed by a bright-eyed elderly lady: it would be a wrench for her to leave, but at her age she wanted to be nearer her children in Kent. In the living room, a fire was burning in the grate. Would they like a cup of tea? Yes, that would be lovely – and with the steaming tea came slices of home-made fruit cake. After their tea, they looked round, trying not to drip too much on the carpets. There were things they would want to change, but this was a home that had been loved, and they could imagine themselves living here, and they would love it too.

'Do you have children?' the lady asked.

'Not yet, but fingers-crossed we will have very soon,' said Mary.

'How wonderful!' said the lady, clapping her gnarled hands. 'The house wants to have children again. I'm so glad you'll be coming here.' She had assumed that Arthur and Mary had already made their decision, and they had. Mary's parents nodded their agreement. Arthur would speak to the agent in the morning.

It was nearly two months before the sale was completed. Over the autumn half-term, Arthur and Mary scoured the second-hand shops for some of the furniture they would need – and treated themselves to a new bed. Mr Warnes lent them his van so they could pick up their purchases and store them at the boatyard until the house was theirs. At last, at the start of November, the big day came. They stood for a moment looking at *Still Waters* – their first home, and one that even Arthur would never quite forget – and Mary cried. Then they took the keys back to Mr Warnes, who helped Arthur load the furniture into his van and drove it round to The Moorings, while Mary followed in the Sunbeam, packed to the gunwales with their possessions. The van was unloaded and furniture arranged; tea was made; goodbyes were said; and finally Arthur and Mary were by themselves in their new, land-locked home. Mary sat down in an armchair. 'You stay there and rest,' said Arthur. 'You shouldn't be overdoing things.'

'I'm not an invalid,' protested Mary, but she had to admit to herself that she was tired and she made no attempt to get up.

'Surely we'll have to change the name?' said Arthur. 'Doesn't The Moorings sound rather silly?'

'They say it's unlucky to change a boat's name.'

'But we're not on a boat now.'

'Well, they're our new moorings and I feel snug here.'

'Suppose,' said Arthur, but it would have to wait, and neither of them would bother about it again.

*

Arthur and Mary settled in quickly at The Moorings, although they missed their watery home. At the weekends they redecorated some of the rooms. Arthur was adamant that Mary should not do too much and under no circumstances should she climb the ladder. Mary complained, but secretly she felt the same. Arthur used his carpentry skills to put up hooks and shelves where they wanted them. He tidied the small garden and they planted bulbs for the spring – snowdrops, crocuses and daffodils. They spent Christmas with Mary's parents and New Year with Grandpa and Grandma, and it was one morning when they were walking along the street in Hartbourne, wrapped up against the cold, that, to Arthur's dismay, they met Sarah. Arthur had that hollow feeling. He had tried his hardest to lay her ghost, but she was like a succubus inveigling herself into his dreams, and now here she was searching him out in real life.

'Hello, Arthur. This is a surprise.' She hugged him tightly. 'And this must be Mary.' She hugged Mary as well. 'It's great to meet you, Mary. I hope you're looking after Arthur – he's one of my most special friends.'

Mary smiled. 'I do my best. It's good to meet you too. Arthur's told me so much about you.' Little does she know, thought Arthur.

'How long are you staying? Perhaps we could all do something together?'

'I'm afraid we're going back tomorrow,' said Arthur, rather too quickly, 'and we shouldn't leave Grandpa and Grandma tonight.'

'Of course not, but how about a walk this afternoon?'

Arthur hesitated, searching for an excuse. 'I'm afraid I'm a bit tired,' said Mary. 'You won't know, but we've got twins on the way.'

'Oh, congratulations, both of you! That's marvellous news. When are you expecting?'

'April, all being well,' said Mary. 'But I'm sure Arthur would be up for a walk. Wouldn't you, Arthur?'

For a moment, Arthur was silent. Oh Mary, you don't know what you're suggesting. A walk with Sarah was an enticing idea – he still found her desperately attractive – but it was something he dreaded because he knew where it might take them. He would always, always, regret that evening at Aunt Dorothy's, but despite the promises he had made to himself he feared he would be too weak to stop it happening again. Perhaps, as dull domesticity had increased its grip, he actually wanted Sarah more than ever. He knew that instead of walking with Sarah he should walk away, but now Mary had made the suggestion, it would be difficult to refuse. So, 'Why not?' he said, summoning up as much enthusiasm as he could. 'As long as Mary doesn't mind.'

After lunch, Arthur called for Sarah at Aunt Dorothy's. 'Shall we walk to our picnic place?' asked Sarah.

Arthur was immediately on the alert. He had not been there since that fateful day, but it had been a favourite place and he would like to see it again. For too long he had looked back on it with dismay, but if he saw it through adult eyes, could he at last assuage his guilt? 'Why not?' he said again, although he knew of all sorts of reasons why not.

In winter, Galleons Lap looked altogether different. The lush trees he remembered were hard and skeletal, and rimed with frost; the surrounding countryside was barren earth, criss-crossed with lines of spiky hedges. It was strange how it was here he had lost his innocence and left his childhood behind. Sarah took his hand and he did not resist. She drew him closer and they kissed, and Arthur knew how much she still meant to him. And they both knew that something else was ending. 'This will always be our special place, Arthur, whatever happens,' said Sarah, and her voice was breaking. ... But I don't think I'll be undressing today.'

So Arthur and Sarah sauntered back to the village. They did not meet Mrs Jones or Alfie and it would not have mattered if they had. Outside Grandpa and Grandma's house they said goodbye, like good friends, not lovers, and Arthur went in to Mary and for tea and toasted crumpets, and although he would not forget Sarah and she would remain a succubus in his dreams, it would be very many years before he would see her again. He was quiet that evening. In a way, Sarah was his alter ego, the free spirit he had half yearned to set free, and he was shutting the door on her. Not only did he want marriage, and Mary, and the twins, more than he wanted Sarah; it was also about the person he was, his good nature shaped and nurtured by his mother, Grandpa and Grandma, and his spirit subdued, for better or for worse, by the bruising 'thou shalt nots' of Sparrowhawk and Burgoyne. And Mary was, after all, something of a free spirit herself – an actress, an artist, a musician – and, without meaning to, he had, since university, too often held her in check. Perhaps, deep down, Mary had understood all this and had let him walk with Sarah so he could make a choice, and perhaps Sarah had understood it too.

*

In January, Mary gave up her job; in February they turned the smallest bedroom into a nursery and Mary's mother came to stay. She helped Mary buy all the things the twins would need: the usual mountain of baby paraphernalia, times two. Everything was rather neutral in colour, since they did not know whether the twins would be boys or girls, or one of each. In March, Mary packed her bag for the hospital. She felt heavy and exhausted, and could not wait for the babies to arrive. In April, in the first week of term when Arthur was taking a history lesson, Mrs Williamson knocked at the door. 'I'm sorry to disturb you, Mr Bright. Do you think I could speak to you for a moment?' Strangely, it reminded Arthur of the day Beaky had knocked at the classroom door when he was attacking the wasp, but this time it was different. 'Mary's just telephoned. She thinks she's going into labour. You'd better go as quickly as you can. I'll make sure your class is looked after. ... Good luck, and love to Mary.'

It all took longer than Arthur had expected, but before midnight two wizened little girls, each with a squelch of dark wet hair, had arrived. They were perfect. It was 23 April, appropriately Shakespeare's birthday. Mary was exhausted and needed to rest, and Arthur went home to telephone her parents. He knew they would not mind being woken up, although he would wait until morning to tell Grandpa and Grandma. Mary's mother answered the phone. There were cries of joy and relief. 'Two girls, I knew it. ... Two girls, Frank. ... Congratulations, Arthur. ... How's Mary? ... Give her our love. ... Let us know when we can visit her. ... How much do they weigh? ... Have you given them names yet? ... Thank you, Arthur. ... Congratulations again. ... You will ring in the morning, won't you? ... Goodnight. ... Lots of love ...'

In the event, the twins' names simply chose themselves. They would call the eldest (by a few minutes) Florence; they would call her sister Maria, after Santa Maria del Fiore, Florence's great cathedral; and one day, when the girls were old enough, they would take them to see the city where their lives began.

*

'Not still looking at that book, are you love? You must know it off-by-heart by now.' Joan has bustled in with a mid-morning mug of coffee for Arthur.

Arthur looks at the mug disapprovingly. 'Isn't Alice in today?'

'It's her day off, lucky girl. ... She's taken a real shine to you, you know.'

Arthur nods. He misses Alice when she does not come.

'Would you like some music, love?'

Arthur winces. 'That would be ... nice,' he says.

'You like your music, don't you?'

'It livens things up ... a bit.' He puts the book down on his knee. Joan switches on the radio, which is tuned to Classic FM. 'There you are. Is that all right, love? It's a bit too highbrow for me, I'm afraid.'

'Thank you,' says Arthur. 'That's … very kind.'

'Anything else you need, love?'

'No, I'll be fine,' says Arthur. 'Isn't … Alice in today?'

'Bye, love. I'll drop in and see you later, then.' Joan disappears on her hectic morning round. Arthur can hear her trolley rattling as she wheels it to the next room. Always in a hurry, love, he thinks. He hopes Alice will be in later. He drinks the milky coffee and lets the music wash over him. It's a lively waltz, one of his favourites, but, try as might, he cannot remember what it is called. He closes his eyes and his book falls to the floor. It is some time later when he is roused by a sharp knock at the door. It is Joan again.

'Had a nice nap, have you, love? You've dropped that book of yours.' She picks it up and hands it to him. 'It's nearly lunchtime. Would you like it in the dining room or in here?' She knows what the answer will be.

'In here, I think … if you don't mind.'

Joan rolls her eyes. It would be much less trouble if he had lunch in the dining room. 'No problem, love, but it'd do you good to get out more often. It'd be much better for you to have some company.'

Arthur has no intention of going to the dining room. 'Perhaps tomorrow. … Is Alice here?'

'It's her day off,' says Joan, a little curtly.

'What a pity,' says Arthur. 'I suppose it's … her day off?'

*

That afternoon Flo comes to visit Arthur. He likes it when Flo comes. He knows she is one of the twins but can't quite make the link between the bundles of childish fun at The Moorings and the grown-up bundles who are now in their fifties.

'You're looking well, Dad.'

'I can't complain.'

'And it's a lovely room you've got.'

'It is, isn't it? I don't know how I found it. ... Are you going to stay tonight? ... You should have told me. ... I don't think I've got anything in ... for your supper.'

'No, Dad, not tonight. I'll have to get back to David and the children, I'm afraid. Another time.'

'That'd be nice. ... Who's David?'

Flo looks out of the window. She finds it hard to engage with her father and his confusions, and she feels ashamed. Marsh View is a misnomer, but, if you look hard enough, you can just make out the salt marshes and what today is the gloomy expanse of the Wash.

'Are you going to ... stay tonight?' asks Arthur.

'No, not tonight, Dad. ... I spoke to Maria yesterday. She sends her love and she's coming to see you soon.'

'How is she? I haven't seen her ... for a long time.'

'She came to see you last week, Dad. She brought you the flowers. Don't you remember?'

Arthur looks at the flowers, red and yellow tulips that are beginning to droop. Of course, he does not remember. 'Have you seen ... my mother?' he asks.

Flo picks up Arthur's book. It is a way to pass the time. She finds the double-page spread of 'The Twins'. She and Maria had especially enjoyed putting this together. It is the story in photographs of their growing up. 'Look at these pictures, Dad, of when we were young.'

Arthur looks. 'One Day Old', taken in the maternity ward. Arthur is holding Flo; Mary is holding Maria. 'That was a ... long time ago.'

'That's me, you're holding,' says Flo.

Arthur looks more closely at the photograph, then at Flo. 'You've changed ... a bit,' he says. 'Are you sure it's ... you?'

Flo sees the old twinkle in his eyes. He is joking. This he does remember. 'We've all changed,' she says.

'Swinging', taken in the garden at The Moorings. The twins are playing on the gaily painted swing Arthur had made, and he is looking on – the proud Dad he once was. 'I built … that swing,' says Arthur.

'First Day at School', taken on the steps at Thorpe Lodge. Mary stands between the twins, holding their hands. They are smart in their new school dresses. 'That's when Maria and I started at Thorpe Lodge,' says Flo.

Arthur closes his eyes for a moment. 'Thorpe Lodge,' he says slowly. 'I worked there … didn't I?'

'For a long time,' says Flo. 'That's where you started teaching.'

Arthur studies the photograph again. 'What happened … to your Mum?' he asks.

Flo ignores the question, hurries him to the next photograph. 'Look at this one, Dad.' 'Skull and Crossbones': the twins must be about eight or nine, a ferocious crew dressed in pirate costumes. Some days they were Skull (Flo) and Crossbones (Maria), flying a gruesome black-and-white flag, and some days Fore and Aft, the nautical twins. It was a holiday on one of Mr Warnes' boats. 'Those holidays were so special,' says Flo, especially when we were older and there were the lugsail dinghies and we learned how to sail. Do you remember Mr Warnes? He was very good to us.'

Arthur looks puzzled. 'I don't think so …'

'He owned the boatyard on Thorpe Island. You used to live on a boat there.' She leafs back through Arthur's book and finds the photograph of *Still Waters*.

A faint smile of recognition. 'We lived on that boat, didn't we? … I don't know what happened to her.'

There are more photographs of the twins: 'At the Funfair', when Arthur and Mary had summoned up courage and taken them to the funfair at Yarmouth, and here they are caught in mid-scream on the big dipper; 'Leavers' Prom' (the twins, in their stunning ball gowns, look so like Mary); 'Graduation' in gowns and hoods (separate photographs – after much soul-searching, the twins had been determined to forge their own identities and, in choosing universities, had gone their separate ways); 'Flo's Wedding' and 'Maria's Wedding' (both at St Andrew's Church, following in Arthur and Mary's footsteps). Flo, a teacher like her father, is married to David, while Maria, who works in local government, has carelessly lost her husband along the way. And 'Grandchildren' (taken on Arthur's sixty-fifth birthday).

Arthur looks quizzically at the scrubbed collection of grandchildren. 'Do I know them?'

'Of course you do. Those two are mine, Henry and Justin. And they're Maria's children. That's Jill and that's John. Doesn't John look like you?' How innocent they look, she thinks. Since then, her boys have been to university, found jobs, left home. Jill has just finished school; John is studying for his A levels.

'Clever clogs. I don't know how you remember their names. … Are you going to stay tonight?'

Flo turns the page and reads aloud. 'I spent ten years at Thorpe Lodge, teaching mainly history and English.' For the most part, Arthur had enjoyed those years. He had quickly proved himself and before long he was teaching history to the older children, preparing them for their entrance exams to senior schools. He had done his best to breathe life into a syllabus that centred on kings and queens and dates, and ignored the more interesting lives of ordinary people. 'Before long, I was invited to give talks at other schools and to local history societies,' continues Flo, 'and I wrote a book about Norwich's past – *Norwich: the Making of a Fine City*.' The book had been launched in the Maddermarket Theatre and there is a photograph of Arthur, smartly suited, signing a copy for the city's gold-chained Lord Mayor.

Flo looks at Arthur. He is no longer concentrating – maybe he is trying to picture Thorpe Lodge – so she turns the page and reads on silently. Grandpa had died in 1973 and when Grandma could no longer cope on her own and The Moorings had become too small for the growing family, Arthur and Mary bought a larger house, Rose Bank, back in Thorpe St Andrew, where Grandma could have her own space. After the twins started school, Mum was offered a part-time job at one of Norwich's auction houses. She enjoyed cataloguing the lots – antiques, jewellery, art, junk – and, with her keen eye, was soon nervously placing commission bids. On a lucky day she would secure a half-valuable item the dealers had missed and before long she was brave enough to have her own stall at one of the city's antiques centres – as it happened, in one of the churches she had helped to restore. In later years she opened a shop in Elm Hill, 'Mary's Antiques and Curios', which attracted dealers and private buyers from miles around.

Flo can picture all this, but she realises, almost with a jolt, how the bare facts she and Maria have assembled may be helpful to Marsh View, but do little to describe their real Dad, either as a husband and a father, or as a teacher whose devotion to his pupils had, for a time, become all-consuming. He was so much more than this, and their life had been far more complicated. Too much sacrifice, she thinks. Mum especially had paid the price, although her antiques were a consolation that delighted her. Flo can just about remember The Moorings, how she and Maria had missed Grandpa after he died, and how Grandma had moved in with them at Rose Bank and looked after them when Mum had cycled off to work; how Rose Bank had smelt of Grandma's baking and of beeswax polish; how Mum had been the wackiest of mothers, always full of fun, always plotting new adventures, always trusting them in their difficult teenage years, always there to listen more than talk; how Dad had come home each evening with stories of his pupils' triumphs and disasters, told sympathetically and with his own wry brand of humour; how they had to try not to make too much noise when he was busy at his desk, and how, as they lay in bed, they could hear the comforting clatter of his typewriter. Above all, she can remember the wild garden at Rose Bank, where in spring there were snowdrops, primroses, daffodils and a magnificent magnolia tree, and in summer the borders were filled with meadow flowers, and the roses bloomed red and pink and white; where they learnt to ride their bicycles on the unkempt lawn; and where they played tomboy games of cowboys and Indians, and built dens beneath the drooping willow tree. She shows Arthur the photograph of Mary's shop – a green fascia with bold gold lettering, a small leaded window, and a door so low you had to stoop to get in and a bell would ring. 'Look, Dad, do you remember Mum's shop with all its treasures? It was like Aladdin's cave. And how you used to sell old books there after you retired?'

Arthur looks up. 'Of course I do. I haven't lost my … memory, you know.' A pause while he tries to process it all. 'What happened to … your Mum?' he asks.

Again, Flo avoids the question. The simple answer is too hideous. But there were other things that happened to Mary, as well as her job at City Hall and her antiques, which are scarcely mentioned in Arthur's book and which Flo can talk to him about. There were her triumphs at the Maddermarket (though she was always too modest to see them as such) – as Irena in Chekhov's *Three Sisters*, as Linda in Arthur Miller's *Death of a Salesman*, and above all and somewhat ironically as Ibsen's tragic heroine, Hedda Gabler, married to boring George Tesman; and there was her enthusiasm for village life, where she was a parish councillor and organiser of events – the pancake race, the Maypole dance, the summer fete, the bonfire night, the bookstall on the Green. What Flo does not mention are the two years at the end of Mary's life when, on top of all this, she cared selflessly for Arthur, struggling to cling onto him as he was sucked deeper into the quicksand of disease and hiding her rage at the injustice of it all.

What is not mentioned either, and what Flo and Maria never suspected, is Mary's far from innocent relationship with Arthur's friend Norman who, after their first candlelit meeting aboard *Still Waters*, had been briefly and unhappily married and then divorced. Having smouldered for a number of years, the relationship was consummated almost unintentionally one Monday morning at The Moorings when Arthur and the twins had left for school, and then continued fitfully whenever the opportunity arose – sometimes, uncomfortably, on a creaking Victorian chaise-longue at the back of Mary's shop, with 'PLEASE WAIT. COMING IN 10 MINUTES' pinned apologetically to the door. After such encounters, did Mary look back on that afternoon on *Still Waters* when Arthur had returned from Hartbourne defensive and ill at ease, not quite elated to learn she was expecting? At the time, she had laughed it off, but was it possible he had been unfaithful too? And, if so, did it in some way excuse her own infidelity? It was not that she was unhappy with Arthur and she did not want to hurt him, but, in those early years of marriage he had been so dedicated to Thorpe Lodge that it was as if the school had become his mistress and she was being neglected; and she was jealous.

*

Like all good things, Arthur's time at Thorpe Lodge did come to an end: it was not of his own volition, but he knew he was stuck in a too comfortable rut. It came as a shock to everyone when Mr Williamson announced his retirement – they had thought he would go on for ever – but a new Head, Mrs Large, was appointed who, according to the letter sent to parents, 'believes in everything Thorpe Lodge stands for and will uphold the values we all cherish as she leads the school on the next stage of its journey'. This was wishful thinking. Almost immediately, Mrs Large, whose ample figure perfectly matched her name, decided the school was too liberal in its outlook. She demanded tighter discipline, more rigour in the teaching and more silence in the classroom. She complained about the time wasted on wishy-washy subjects like drama, music and art. She objected to the playtimes – which, she declared, should be constructive and not 'this noisy free-for-all'. She failed to understand that parents had chosen Thorpe Lodge because of its relaxed ways and broad curriculum; and, since she ignored their complaints, they began to take their children away. Arthur, along with his colleagues, despaired at what was happening, but it was the push he needed and by one of those happy coincidences he learned that Spinney Hill, a school a few miles west of Norwich, was looking for a history teacher.

Spinney Hill was run on the same wavy lines as Thorpe Lodge: a progressive school, as some said approvingly; a crank school, in the opinion of others. Arthur liked its lively atmosphere, the lack of pretention and the natural good manners of its high-spirited pupils. He liked its motto, 'Courage and Compassion'. How different it was from Sparrowhawk and Burgoyne, and from what Thorpe Lodge was rapidly becoming. How the Cholmondeley-Robinsons would have despised it. He was sure he could be happy there. Although he had no experience of teaching older children, his reputation as a historian and author, and an outstanding reference from Mr Williamson, stood him in good stead and, after two gruelling interviews and a nerve-jangling observed lesson, he was offered the position. It was a bonus that Spinney Hill had its own junior department and, since Arthur and Mary no longer believed in the direction Thorpe Lodge had taken under Mrs Large, they decided the twins should move there with him along with several of their classmates.

Arthur was to spend the rest of his long teaching career at Spinney Hill and it was the most important thing in his life – more important than Thorpe Lodge and often (he admitted to himself guiltily) more important than even Mary and the twins. 'Tell me about Spinney Hill,' says Alice (yet again) one day, after she has tidied the room and put away his laundry. 'You gave your life to that school, didn't you?'

'Nearly thirty years. … I often wonder if I gave … too much.'

I Am Arthur Bright

In Arthur's book there are numerous photographs of Spinney Hill. Together they look at the first photograph: 'With the Twins on our First Day at Spinney Hill'. The twins are grinning from ear to ear. Arthur has forgotten to smile. 'You look far more nervous than the twins,' laughs Alice.

'I think I was. It was a bit … daunting at first and they all tried to … play me up … testing me out … but they weren't much different from … the younger ones.'

'And where's this, Arthur?'

He peers at the picture. 'I'm not sure. … Mm. … Yes … the Roman Town at Caistor. … I used to take the first form there … We went out on lots of trips.' Arthur had taken Norfolk and its history to his heart, and as well as teaching his pupils what they needed for their examinations, he would tell them about the wool trade, the cloth trade, the Hanseatic league, the Peasants' Revolt and the Battle of North Walsham, and how in 1549 Robert Kett led a rebellion on Mousehold Heath outside Norwich and was executed for his trouble. The boys generally enjoyed the executions more than the girls.

'And this one?' Alice is pointing to another photograph: 'Roman Holiday', taken in front of the Coliseum in Rome – Arthur with a party of schoolchildren, and with Mary and the twins as well.

'I think you know … where that is,' says Arthur (although at first Alice had not known). We used to take the children … to Italy in the holidays. … Sometimes Rome … sometimes Pompeii.'

'They were so lucky,' says Alice. 'We didn't go on school trips. I'd love to go to Italy.'

Arthur looks at her in a fatherly way. 'Perhaps I'll take you … one day. But … I'm not sure Mary would let me.'

There is a photograph of Arthur with two of his pupils, a boy and a girl who had won scholarships to Oxford, and there are extracts from the letters of thanks Arthur had saved and treasured, and the twins had discovered:

Thank you, Mr Bright, for all you've done to help me over the past two sixth-form years - and making sure we 'got it'. I wouldn't have gained my place at Cambridge without you. (Susan Hall)

Dear Sparky
Thanks a million! Youre the best teacher ever. I know I was never your easyest pupil but I wont forget how much you helped me. The trip to Rome smashed it. (Dylan)

Dear Mr Bright
I am really grateful for your inspiring lessons and for all your extra help and encouragement. I am going to miss you - and so will Spinney Hill. (Jane S.)

The letters meant much to Arthur. He regretted he had never written to thank his own special teachers, Mr Penfold, Mr Castle and Dr Robinson, to express his gratitude. He owed them a lot. He must have changed so many lives, thought Alice, and look at him now. It's so unfair.

There is another photograph of Arthur giving the prizes on Speech Day at Spinney Hill. It was in 2002, when the headmaster was taken ill and the governors asked Arthur to take over as Acting Headmaster. He stood in for nearly a year, but never enjoyed it. It took him out of the classroom too much and he had no appetite for the bureaucracy, the budgets, the letters, the awkward parents, the recalcitrant staff, and the changed relationship with the children. No, it was very flattering, but he had no interest in applying for the permanent post. With considerable relief, he returned to the common room, but he noticed how his colleagues and the children treated him differently, holding him more at a distance. It was only a subtle change but, without anyone meaning it, a spell had been broken.

Arthur retired three years later, at the age of sixty. Although no-one saw it apart from Mary, his old enthusiasm had waned. He did not like the new young headmaster, smooth as a statue, slim as a snake, who was not a Spinney Hill person at all: he had publicly criticised Arthur's 'sloppy' *inter regnum* and had upbraided him for being too easy-going ('They think they've got you twisted round their sticky little fingers, Mr Bright'; 'Yes, Headmaster, but I know I've got them twisted round mine, and look at the history results'). Arthur had loved Spinney Hill, but he saw no point in hanging around like the unwanted guest at a wedding and there were other things he could do while he still had the energy. He would like to get back to writing and he had a growing interest in antiquarian books, which he might just turn into a business: Mary had suggested he could have some space in her shop. So the last photograph of the Spinney Hill years is of Arthur's final assembly: 'Three Cheers for Sparky'. The parents had organised a collection and the headmaster is presenting Arthur with an original watercolour of Norwich market. His oily smile does not quite mask his considerable satisfaction and relief. In the background, the pupils are waving their arms: 'Three cheers for Sparky … Hip, hip hooray! … And one for luck!' As Arthur walked out into the sunshine, they were still singing. 'For he's a jolly good fellow, And so say all of us.' Put that in your pipe, Headmaster, he thought. After so long, he had become part of the fabric of the place, but he was never invited back.

Alice can see that Arthur is listening to the cheers again; his eyes are glistening and a stray tear is rolling down his cheek.

*

The last two pages of Arthur's story tell mainly of a contented semi-retirement. He wrote three more books about Norfolk's history, all of which were notable for their lightness of touch and the way in which they told stories. It has to be said (although Maria had been too tactful to say it) that Mary resented the books. They tied Arthur to his laptop, which had replaced his typewriter, and he had no more time for recreation than before. She believed, with some justification, that she was still taking second place and as a matter of principle she never read any of them. There were times when she even resented the marriage. Would her life have been more exciting with Norman? Probably not. Norman was not unlike Arthur and, to start with at least, she had seen their affair mainly as an act of rebellion. Once her marriage to Arthur had been exciting – *Still Waters* had been exciting, and The Moorings, where the twins had been such joyous bundles of fun. Once they had been deeply in love; no, they probably still were, but in a different, sadder way. Arthur had been unfailingly caring, reliable and kind – the qualities which had so attracted her half a century ago – but she wished that he could, just once, have broken free from the conventional life of a schoolmaster and taken the whole family off on some wild adventure. Who knows where it might have led? It was infuriating how he had become so stuck in his ways; but they were, by most measures, good ways, so perhaps it was unreasonable of her to complain.

The research for his books did take Arthur and Mary on regular day trips and the odd weekend away, but rarely out of East Anglia. It was all so uninspiring. Mary hoped he would one day turn his heretical ideas on the British Empire into a book, so they could travel to more distant parts. She yearned for new experiences – to see the Taj Mahal, go on an African safari, swim off Bahaman beaches – but it never happened and the few foreign holidays they took were confined to Europe. Like Mary, Arthur had long ago fallen in love with Italy. More than once they returned to Florence and they found it hard to resist the splendours of Rome, by now familiar after so many Spinney Hill expeditions, and the beauty of the Amalfi coast. They celebrated their golden wedding in Venice, their favourite city, where they are photographed in a gondola and amid the crowds and pigeons of St Mark's Square, but it was a shame that in recent years the gargantuan cruise ships had arrived, disgorging passengers in their thousands and washing away the city's fragile foundations.

Mary continued to run her shop, although now it was open less often. She remained a stalwart of the Norwich Players – 'It seems I'm only fit for character parts these days,' she complained. Arthur's interest in the theatre, which, after all, had only been sparked by an interest in Mary, gradually flickered and died, but he was always on the look-out for antiquarian books and first editions with an East Anglian flavour. He loved these books, with their musty smell, their mysterious inscriptions and marginalia, and their yellowed pages, and he tried to imagine the stories that lay behind them. He filled more and more shelves in Mary's shop (with a twinge of regret, she had to move the creaking chaise longue to accommodate them) and this, at least, was a shared interest. He enjoyed talking with customers and was almost sad if he made a sale. It was like saying goodbye to a valued friend. The inevitable sadnesses of old age – the deaths of Grandma and of Mary's parents – go unrecorded in Arthur's story. Maria had pondered how to deal with Arthur's dementia and the last tortuous years at Rose Bank: they are a blank in Arthur's mind, but they cannot be left out. In the end, she had decided to meet them head-on, because that is what Arthur would have wanted: 'In 2019 I was diagnosed with Alzheimer's disease and life became very difficult, especially for Mary,' she wrote. 'Mary insisted we should carry on just as before, and for a time we did, with a memorable holiday in Malta. [In 'memorable' Maria has chosen the wrong word: Arthur has forgotten all about it.] Then the Covid epidemic, which swept the world soon afterwards, confined us to Rose Bank for long periods and my condition worsened, but we still managed a week on the Norfolk Broads and some enjoyable days out.' There are photographs of Arthur and Mary looking out over Malta's Grand Harbour, of cruising on the Broads, and of other special days in the dying of the light, before the shattering final sentence, which hides much more than it tells, and is not the end of the story at all: 'After

Mary's tragic death, it was time for me to leave our home at Rose Bank and move nearer to Flo. I now live at Marsh View at Salthouse, near Sheringham, where I can enjoy the sights and sounds of the sea.' Enjoying the sights and sounds of the sea is disingenuous, but it reassures Flo and Maria, who would like to think it is true.

V

Muddle

Looking back, Mary could see how Arthur was no longer the man he was, though at the time the changes had been gradual and so unremarked. When he spoke, he had grown more hesitant, searching for words. Then he had begun to repeat himself, asking the same question over and over again. He had started to lose things and to miss appointments. On social occasions, even with friends, he had become quiet and withdrawn. But that summer, on two particular days, the changes came jarringly into focus. It was not just that Arthur was getting old. On the surface, he was turning into a different person altogether.

*

The first of those days was Mary's seventy-fifth birthday. They had celebrated with a meal at their favourite Italian restaurant. It had the bustling atmosphere of the tiny trattoria they had discovered in Venice on the special holiday that marked their golden wedding. After their meal – for old times' sake they had both chosen the seafood risotto and the tiramisu – they had gone to the Theatre Royal. It was Agatha Christie's usual fare: murder in an isolated country house, a collection of back-biting suspects, each with a half-plausible motive, and that annoying Belgian detective on hand finally to unmask the villain.

'Well, who was the murderer?' asked Arthur as he was driving them home.

'Oh, Arthur, did you fall asleep again? It was the Major. But I never thought it would be him.'

'In the library with Miss Scarlett, I suppose. I couldn't work it out at all. And what was the name of the detective?'

'It was Hercule Poirot,' said Mary in her best Belgian accent. 'It's always Poirot and his "little grey cells". An arrogant little man. I think Miss Marple is much more down-to earth.'

They were approaching the roadworks near the station. The works had been going on for months, but in the dark they looked entirely different. Arthur would never know what it was that confused him. There were the array of yellow diversion signs, the flashing cones, and the men in their orange hi-vis jackets standing languidly under the arc lights. Or was he still thinking of the Major and Poirot, and about why his mind was becoming a fog? 'Arthur!' exclaimed Mary, rousing him from his reverie, 'Look out! You're in the wrong lane!'

And suddenly there were headlights coming towards them, horns sounding, brakes screeching, people gesticulating. Somehow, Arthur managed to stop the car. He was shaking. Mary reached across and switched on the hazard lights. The oncoming traffic slowed and managed to weave its way past. A workman came over and Mary wound down the window. 'Bloody stupid,' he said loudly, making himself heard above the rumble of machinery. 'What the hell were you playing at, pal? Lucky you didn't cause a bloody accident.' He looked across at Arthur, who had covered his face, and softened. 'I think perhaps you ought to take over the driving, madam.'

'I ... d ... didn't mean ...' stammered Arthur.

The workman stopped the traffic. Mary climbed out, opened Arthur's door, and helped him round to the passenger seat. 'Thank you,' she said to the workman. I'm so, so sorry.'

'No probs, madam. No harm done, thank goodness.' He moved some cones so Mary could make a three-point turn. She steeled herself not to make a mistake.

'That must have been my most exciting birthday ever,' said Mary later, as she made them steaming mugs of hot chocolate. 'Those roadworks were so disorientating. I suppose it could have happened to anyone.' But she was humouring him. She knew it could only have happened to Arthur.

*

The second day Mary would never forget was a Wednesday. It was about a week after her birthday. She was surprised that Arthur could barely recall their dicing with death at the roadworks, an episode which had so firmly imprinted itself on her mind. They had been fortunate to escape unscathed. It was obvious Arthur needed help, but she could not decide on the right thing to do. She had not dared to tell anyone what had happened, not even Flo and Maria.

There was an unseasonable chill in the air and a light rain was falling when Arthur set off after breakfast, as he always did, to walk the half mile or so to Mr Shastri's convenience store to buy a newspaper. He liked to keep up with the news, however depressing it might be, and the puzzles near the back would keep him busy in the afternoon, especially since lately they had been making them more difficult. It was a pleasant stroll, even in the wet – down the tree-lined avenue, turn right by the postbox on the corner, and just across the road was Shastri's. Arthur enjoyed the fresh air and the exercise, but today, as every day, he was infuriated by the people he passed. He recognised them, of course, yet none of them was in any way familiar. There were the teenagers on their reluctant way to school. Some, the untucked-shirt brigade, pushed and shoved in irritating horseplay, and too often he had to step into the road to avoid them; others walked by themselves, staring intently at their phones; and others still, the head-phoned zombies, looked vacantly ahead. Then there were the bleary-eyed mothers, also glued to their phones and ignoring their grizzling toddlers, and the dog-walkers, who talked to each other but to no-one else, carrying, with some embarrassment, little plastic bags of poo. Arthur, it seemed, was invisible to them all. These days he only mumbled the occasional 'good morning' and he dared not smile politely at the schoolgirls or the young mothers in case they mistook his intentions. Was it all a simple matter of bad manners; or was it something more fundamental and disturbing – a shrinking, in this different world of texts and posts, from even passing human contact? And was he, too, being infected? 'Look at me! I am Arthur Bright! I am here!' he wanted to exclaim; but instead he cast down his eyes and continued on his way. He waved to Mrs Jenkins, an old friend who lived in the next street, but lately she had been in a rush and did not have the time to stop and chat. 'I don't know why Mrs Jenkins has suddenly got so busy,' he would say to Mary with monotonous regularity.

However, at the shop Arthur's mood lifted. 'Good morning, Mr Bright,' said the always beaming Mr Shastri. 'It will be another, nice day, I think. The sun will soon be shining again.' For Mr Shastri, the sun would always be shining or about to shine, which was one of the secrets of his thriving business. Yes, it would be a nice day after all, agreed Arthur as he paid for his paper and, as a self-indulgent treat, his favourite chocolate bar. For a few minutes they talked of this and that, before Arthur, pleased they had put the world a little bit to rights and conscious of the queue stirring restlessly behind him, went on his way. Mary would be worrying where he had got to. He knew she worried about him more and more, but really there was no need.

And Mary was beginning to worry. It was ten o'clock and Arthur was always back by then. She wondered if he'd taken the long way home or made a detour to the river. At half past ten, he was still not back. Perhaps he'd met Mr Jenkins, an old colleague from Thorpe Lodge all those years ago, and gone back for a coffee. At eleven o'clock, she wondered if he'd been in an accident. She put on her anorak and took Arthur's customary route. 'No,' said, Mr Shastri, when Mary arrived, out of breath, at the shop. 'Arthur came at his right time, regular as clockworks. He was his usual happy, happy self. Do not be troubled, Mrs Bright. The sun is shining. He has luckily met someone and forgotten the time. You must make him carry a phone. He is surely at your house now and he is demanding where you are. That would be funny.' Mr Shastri beamed.

Mary was not sure whether it was Mr Shastri's not altogether perfect English or his unquenchable and beaming optimism that annoyed her more. Arthur was surely not at home and it was not at all funny. She phoned Flo at school and left a message. Flo phoned back at breaktime: 'Don't worry, Mum. I'm sure he'll be back with some wild story. Call me when he is.' She phoned Maria, by nature more of a worrier, but she lived a long way away. 'Oh gosh, Mum. What on earth can have happened? Let me know when he turns up. Or do you want me to drive over? I can take the afternoon off if you like.' At midday she phoned the police, who were complacent and condescending. Obviously they did not think Arthur counted as a missing person, or not yet anyway. 'We'll keep an eye out for him, Mrs Bright. You stay at home in case he contacts you or there's any news. … Just let us know when he shows up.' She did not know if he would show up. She felt helpless and afraid.

After another hour, which seemed like ten, a car drew up outside. From the window, Mary saw Arthur climbing out sheepishly and Bill Chalmers from the Bridge Club walking up the path with him. She hurried to the door, opened it, and burst into tears. 'Nothing to worry about, Mary,' said Bill reassuringly. 'I bumped into Arthur in Riverside Park and we've had a good catch-up, haven't we, Arthur?' Riverside Park, Mary knew, was some way away: clearly Arthur had had quite an adventure.

'Riverside Park!' exclaimed Mary. 'How on earth did you get there, Arthur?'

'I just walked. I thought I needed a good walk.'

'I'll leave you two to it,' said Bill tactfully. 'It was good to catch up with you, Arthur.'

'I can't thank you enough, Bill,' said Mary. 'It's so far out of your way.'

'My pleasure, Mary. I'll see you both at bridge on Monday.' And, with a cheery wave, he was gone.

Mary watched Bill drive away. 'Come on, Arthur, let's take your coat off and you can tell me what happened.'

'I don't think there's anything to tell, actually,' protested Arthur as Mary fussed over him. 'I just went for a longer walk today.'

Mary telephoned the twins and the police to say the wanderer had returned. She would walk round to tell Mr Shastri later.

*

When Arthur stepped out of Mr Shastri's shop, he had tucked the newspaper under his arm and set off for home. The rain was stopping and the sun was breaking through the lowering clouds. He agreed that Mr Shastri was right and it would be a nice day after all. There were things in the garden to be done and, making a mental list of the tasks ahead, he quickened his pace. Except he had absent-mindedly turned left instead of right and, by the time he had finished his list, he was not entirely sure where he was. He should have been home by now, but he half recognised the streets and there was no need to worry. He ran through his list again. There was a window to be repaired in the greenhouse; there was the tiresome business of weeding; there were some roses that needed spraying; and, if by this afternoon the grass had dried, he would mow the lawn. He hummed to himself – one of those hymn tunes he had learned at Sparrowhawk and which had afterwards livened up the assemblies at Thorpe Lodge and Spinney Hill. He hadn't been concentrating, but he must be home soon. And he was. There was a moment of relief, followed at once by a moment of panic. He was standing outside The Moorings.

How had he managed to land up here? Surely he could simply retrace his steps: it was, after all, the way he had walked every day to Thorpe Lodge. But now, in his horror and confusion, his sense of direction deserted him entirely.

Which way should he go? He thought right – it looked more familiar. And so he became lost in the labyrinth of roads, with no ball of thread to help him find his way back. He started to worry and he knew Mary would be worrying too. He should have brought his phone with him – Mary was always telling him he should – but he hated phones and he wasn't sure how to work it anyway. Until now, he had never seen the need to learn. So, by chance, he arrived at the gates of Riverside Park. He knew the Park: when they had lived at The Moorings, he had often come here with Mary and the twins. He could find a bench and rest his legs for a while, and there might be someone he could ask for help. He sat on a graffiti-scrawled bench, ate the chocolate bar, and tried to sort out the muddle in his head. It was not just his memory that was the problem. Everything was becoming more difficult and he knew he was losing control. He looked at the children playing contentedly and after a while he began to doze. It was here that Bill Chalmers, who happened to live nearby, recognised him and sensed that something was wrong. In fact, he had sensed for some time that something was wrong with Arthur. Bill shook him gently. 'Hello, Arthur.'

Arthur looked up, not sure for a moment where he was. 'It's Bill, isn't it? What are you … doing here?'

'I ought to ask you the same, Arthur. This isn't your neck of the woods.'

'I decided I needed a walk. I wanted the … exercise.' He raised his eyes nervously. 'It just turned out longer … than I planned.'

'Well, you look as if you've walked far enough for one day. Let me give you a lift home. It won't take a minute to get the car.'

'I'm quite all right, thank you,' lied Arthur, relieved that help had arrived from an unexpected quarter. 'But if it isn't too much trouble? … I'd rather lost track of time and Mary will have expected me long ago.'

'No trouble at all, Arthur. You just wait here.'

Arthur struggled to his feet. 'At least I can come with you to the car.'

'If you're sure.' Bill had the good sense not to dent Arthur's pride further.

*

'You've given me such a fright, Arthur,' said Mary, helping him with his coat. 'I didn't know what had happened to you. I even phoned the police.'

'The police? You shouldn't have done that. I just went for a walk.'

'You sit down, and I'll get us some lunch. You must be starving.'

'Don't fuss,' said Arthur. 'I had a chocolate bar.' He had noticed how over the last few months Mary had become more and more fussy. The last thing he needed was her fussing. He might sometimes get in a muddle, but he wasn't stupid. He was quite capable of looking after himself.

'I've got half a packet of smoked salmon in the fridge and I'll make some scrambled egg.'

'I'm not hungry,' said Arthur.

'I'm sure you'll want it when it's in front of you.' Mary busied herself in the kitchen with so many thoughts racing through her head – not only about Arthur's expedition that morning, but also about their near accident on the way back from the theatre and his increasing forgetfulness over the past few months. She laid the small table and set down the salmon and eggs. After a long silence, she said, 'What did you actually get up to this morning, Arthur? And how on earth did you land up in Riverside Park?'

'I told you. I went for a walk. In fact, I went to see where we lived at The Moorings.' He pushed the egg around his plate but made no attempt to eat. He looked at Mary, trying to be angry, but suddenly his face crumpled. 'I don't know what's happening to me, Mary.'

'Oh, Arthur.' She got up from the table, went to him, put an arm around his shoulders and held him tightly. Arthur had become unused to such a physical gesture – they were no longer that sort of couple – but he found it strangely comforting. For a minute or two neither of them spoke. 'I'm sure we can sort things out,' said Mary. In reality she was not sure at all.

Arthur picked at his food. They talked about the garden and the children, but not about the morning's debacle. Mary made coffee. Arthur opened his newspaper but could not concentrate. 'I do think you should see Dr Thomas,' said Mary. 'There must be something he can do to help with your muddle.' Dr Thomas was their family doctor and they had known him for some time.

'I don't think there's a cure for muddle. I'll just have to be more careful. That's all there is to it.' He went back to his newspaper.

'But it wouldn't do any harm, would it?'

'I suppose not.' Arthur looked up, half smiled at Mary and looked away. 'But if it's what you want, you can make an appointment. As long as you promise to come with me.' He knew she was right.

It took Mary some time to negotiate the new booking system at the surgery and she had no intention of discussing Arthur's muddle with the brusque receptionist. It would sound trivial and she couldn't claim it was an emergency. When it was obvious Mary was not for turning, the reluctant Ms Brusque agreed grudgingly that Dr Thomas would be able to squeeze them in on the following Friday. Mary could remember the time when old Dr Davis would have seen them on the same day, and if one of the twins had been ill, he would have made a house call, even at night. These days it was a victory to get an appointment at all.

The waiting room at the surgery was unwelcoming. Tired notices about illnesses and vaccinations, and volunteers needed for this and that. Warnings about aggressive behaviour. Grubby copies of *Country Life* and *What Car* long out-of-date. Hard chairs. Noisy youngsters. Patients looking glumly or enquiringly at each other. Germs breeding visibly in the stuffy heat. After a while, and twenty minutes after their appointment was due, they heard a loud 'Next Patient Please' over the loudspeaker and 'Mr Arthur Bright to Room 2' flashed up on the screen. It was a long time since Arthur had been to the doctor. There were eyes staring at him accusingly: wasn't he jumping the queue? He felt self-conscious and humiliated.

In Room 2, Dr Thomas listened carefully and tapped on his keyboard. He did his best to be reassuring. 'Let's not jump to any conclusions, Arthur. There could be all sorts of treatable things causing the muddle – an infection, maybe, or an under-active thyroid – and we'll rule these out before we even think about dementia. That would be a real bugger and I'm afraid there's not that much we can do about it.'

Arthur and Mary looked at each other. 'Dementia' and 'Not that much we can do about it' were the only words they took in. Dr Thomas had been less than tactful.

'Ask at Reception on your way out,' said Dr Thomas, 'and they'll arrange a blood test for you with the nurse. And we'd better have a urine sample, too. They'll give you a pot. I'll be in touch as soon as we get the results.' He stood up to show the consultation was over. 'Take things carefully, Arthur, and let's hope it's not the worst.' Dr Thomas and Arthur shook hands. 'Good to see you both. Still enjoying retirement? Shop doing well, Mary?' Arthur and Mary let the pleasantries flow over their heads. They picked up a pot from Ms Brusque, who held it out delicately between finger and thumb, as if it were something unpleasant. Arthur smuggled it discreetly into his pocket.

Blood was taken, the pot returned – Ms Brusque looked even

more disapproving – and two weeks later they were back at the surgery for the results. 'Come along in,' greeted Dr Thomas, 'and have a seat.' He turned to Arthur. 'How are you, Arthur?'

'I rather think that's for you to tell me, Doctor,' said Arthur. It was resigned, not malicious.

Dr Thomas looked to his screen to provide the unwelcome answers. The computer says ... He was only the messenger. 'Well, I can see the news is good and bad, Arthur. All the tests show you're in tip-top physical condition for someone of your age.'

'Well, that's the good news,' said Arthur, 'but let's cut to the chase, shall we? What's the bad?' It was not like him to be impatient. He knew what was coming.

Dr Thomas leant back in his chair and smiled unconvincingly. At moments like these, he found it difficult to tell the truth. He would leave it to someone else to do that. 'To be honest, Arthur, I'm not sure I know, but I think we should refer you to the Memory Clinic at the hospital. I'll get in touch with them and they'll contact you shortly. They'll most likely book you in for a scan and some more tests, and then fix an appointment for you with the specialist.' He paused. 'I'm afraid these days "shortly" can mean some time.'

'So you're passing the buck, aren't you?' said Mary. She had always been more forthright than Arthur. She liked Dr Thomas, but she didn't like his shillyshallying. Each of them knew what he was trying not to say. Her life, like Arthur's, was falling apart.

'Let's just wait and see what they diagnose,' soothed Dr Thomas. 'They're very good at the Clinic.'

'Thank you, Doctor,' said Arthur. 'But I think the answer's pretty clear. I seem to remember you saying dementia's a bugger and there isn't much anyone can do about it.'

Doctor Thomas looked embarrassed, changed the subject, asked if they were taking a holiday this year. Arthur and Mary listened to none of it. They were already moving towards the door.

It was two weeks before a letter arrived from the Memory Clinic, another two weeks before the scan at the hospital ('Frying what's left of my brain,' said Arthur) and a further week before they carried out the tests. For all that time Arthur and Mary skirted round the subject. In the daylight hours, Arthur was unusually quiet, but things carried on as they had always done and Mary thought it best not to interfere. She worried each time he went for his newspaper, but he had become more careful and, to her relief, had always managed to return home safely. 'Do you mind if I come with you today?' she would sometimes ask. She did not want to shake his confidence, but she was conscious there would come a time when she would have to go with him everywhere, and it might be best if he became used to it. It seemed to Mary that Arthur was growing even more forgetful, but she hoped it was only her heightened sense of awareness which made her notice it. In bed, in the quiet of the night, lying side by side, they were alone with their imaginings and regrets. Arthur knew the disease would steal not just his life but his whole self, and what saddened him more was the effect it would have on the twins and the grandchildren, and the heavy burden he would become to Mary. For her part, free-spirited Mary dwelt in the darkness on her shattered dreams. She had hoped the next few years would be filled with travel and adventure, and all the other things that Arthur's teaching and writing had cramped and put on hold. Instead she could only think how before long she would become his nurse. Fifty years ago she had made a vow to stay loyal to Arthur 'in sickness and in health' and, although she had not always succeeded, she had only strayed a little. However much she hated the idea, she would make the best of it.

*

It was Mary who drove Arthur to the Memory Clinic, which was in a separate, white-painted building some distance from the main hospital. Arthur had spent a great deal of time before the appointment preparing himself, just as he had once prepared his pupils meticulously for their exams. He had googled the sort of test he would be given and had tried to memorise the answers. But memorising was the problem. 'I just can't manage it, Mary,' he burst out, throwing down his notebook, and putting his head in his hands.

'You're not meant to manage it, Arthur,' said Mary. 'It's not an exam. They're trying to find out if there's anything wrong with you and it'll be a waste of time if you try to disguise it.' Secretly she hoped he would disguise it, so for a little longer they could carry on as if nothing were amiss.

The waiting room at the Clinic was much like the one at the doctor's surgery, but there was only one other person there, no screens or loudspeakers, and no cloud of germs. They talked meaninglessly about nothing of consequence until a young lady emerged to usher them into her office. Her long, dark hair curled over her shoulders and she wore dangly ear-rings, gold-rimmed spectacles and a small gold ring in her nose. Arthur recited Edward Lear's 'The Owl and the Pussycat' to himself: 'With a ring at the end of his nose, his nose ...' If pressed, Mary would have described the lady's long dress as 'bohemian'; she rather liked it. 'Mr and Mrs Bright?' enquired the young lady pleasantly. Do come in. I'm so sorry if I've kept you.' She had not, in fact, kept them at all. 'I'm Joanna,' she said. Her manner was friendly, but she knew Arthur was from a generation that preferred to be addressed formally. 'Do have a seat.' She beckoned them to a large, round table. She sat down at the table herself. There was the inevitable laptop, a small pile of papers, and a notepad. 'Now, Mr Bright, can you tell me what's been going on with you?'

'Well, nothing, really,' said Arthur. 'I suppose I've just been forgetting a few things.'

Joanna glanced at Mary, who looked away, and made a note. 'Well, that doesn't sound so bad. But obviously Dr Thomas is a bit worried about you and we're here to see if we can help.'

'I don't want to be a …' said Arthur, his voice trailing away.

Joanna made another note. 'Of course you don't. But tell me some of the things that have been happening.'

Little by little, Joanna teased out from Arthur and Mary the difficulties of the last few months: the everyday forgetfulness, the growing introspection, the good days and bad days, Arthur's concern for his long-dead mother, the hair-raising escapade in the car, and the unplanned jaunt to Riverside Park which had brought matters to a head. She listened carefully and wrote copiously. 'Thank you,' she said. 'That's given me a very full picture. Now, Mr Bright, would it be all right if I asked you a few questions to test your memory? It shouldn't take very long.'

'Well, yes,' said Arthur, 'That's … what I'm here for, isn't it?' In a strange way, he was rather looking forward to it.

'Splendid!' said Joanna, and then, 'Do you know what year it is, Mr Bright?'

Arthur stifled a laugh. He had prepared for this one. 'Yes,' he answered confidently. 'It's 2019.'

'And the season?'

Arthur looked out of the window, where the rain was pouring down. 'It looks like … autumn,' he said, although at the back of his mind he was not sure if that was right. 'Or is it summer?'

'And the month?'

Arthur pondered for a bit. 'August.' And then, 'But with all this … rain I think it must be … September … or … October. I … ought to know.'

'Well, what month do you think it is?'

Arthur looked flustered.

'There's no hurry. Take your time, Mr Bright.'

Arthur looked again at the rain. 'Probably … September. Yes, September.'

Damn the rain, seethed Mary silently. He knows very well it's summer and it's August.

'And can you remember the date, Mr Bright?'

Arthur had never been good at dates, except the history ones drummed into him at Sparrowhawk and Burgoyne. He had tried to make a mental note of the appointment, but it had slipped his mind. After a time, 'I'm not sure about that one' he said. 'But I know it's Wednesday. It's the day we put the dustbins out.'

Joanna nodded approvingly and wrote something down. More questions followed. The country; the county; the town. No problems there. Arthur and Mary had lived in the area for fifty years. Joanna leant back in her chair and looked around. 'Do you know what building we're in?' she asked.

'Oh yes.' It had all been easier than Arthur had anticipated and this was another question he'd prepared for. 'We're at the Memory Clinic at the … hospital.' He paused. He didn't want to be here and he suddenly felt he was being patronised. 'I thought you'd know that since you work here.' Mary glared at him, willing him to behave.

'I suppose I should.' Joanna laughed and was quite unperturbed. 'Now, Mr Bright, I'm going to name three objects and I want you to repeat them to me. Then I want you to try hard to really remember them, because I'm going to ask you about them again in a few minutes. Ball … Car … Man.'

'Ball … Car … Man,' said Arthur, although he was not sure if 'Man' was an object and he noticed the split infinitive. What sort of question is that, he thought.

'Good. But make sure you remember them.' She looked down at the paper in front of her. 'Can you spell the word "World" for me?'

'W … O … R … L … D,' said Arthur confidently. The Sparrowhawk spelling lists had not deserted him.

'Excellent. And can you spell it backwards?'

Arthur pondered for a while. 'D … R … L … O … W. No, that's

not right. D ... L ... O ... R ... W.'

'Sure?' said Joanna.

'Sure,' said Arthur.

Mary winced. It was the sort of answer that a year or two ago Arthur would never have got wrong.

'Now, Mr Bright,' said Joanna. 'Can you tell me the three objects I asked you to remember?'

Arthur looked mystified. 'Three objects? ... I don't remember any ...'

'Never mind,' said Joanna after what seemed an age. 'Let's carry on. Not many questions to go.' She pointed to her watch. 'What am I pointing at Mr Bright?'

Arthur laughed. 'I can still recognise a watch!'

'And this?' She held up her pencil.

Arthur laughed again. 'And I can still recognise a ... pencil when I see it!'

The questions went on and by the end of them Arthur was feeling rather pleased with himself. Perhaps the future would not be so bleak after all. Joanna showed them out. 'We'll be in touch with an appointment for you to see the consultant. Take care, Mr Bright. It's been a pleasure to meet you both.'

'Well, Mary,' said Arthur, as they were driving home, 'that wasn't nearly as bad as I'd expected, and what a nice young lady. We pulled the wool over her eyes, didn't we? Let's have lunch out to celebrate.'

'Yes, let's. That nice café isn't far from here.' Mary did not want to deflate him. 'Ball ... Car ... Man', she muttered under her breath. 'Do you know what month it is, Arthur?'

Arthur looked across at her. 'August, of course. Why do you ask?'

*

At last, towards the end of September, there was an appointment for Arthur to see Dr Patel, the consultant psychiatrist at the Memory

Clinic. It was the day Arthur and Mary had been dreading. If anything, Arthur had become more forgetful and he was more irritable as well. Mary had the patience of a saint, but even saints can sometimes boil over with frustration. They were both certain what the diagnosis would be, but they dared not admit it, even to each other. They sat in the same waiting room as before. Joanna came out of her office to greet another patient. She recognised Arthur and Mary. 'It's good to see you again. I expect you've come to see Dr Patel. I'm sure he won't be long.'

She knows exactly what he's going to say, thought Mary.

Another door opened and a man in a grey, pin-striped suit approached them. 'Mr and Mrs Bright? It's a pleasure to meet you both. He beamed at them. He reminded Arthur of the beaming Mr Shastri.

'Dr Alzheimer, I presume?' said Arthur, shaking hands with Dr Patel.

Dr Patel had heard the joke many times before. 'I'm afraid not, Mr Bright. I'm Dr Patel. Dr Alzheimer left us some time ago, I believe.' He turned towards Mary. 'And this is your wife?'

'Yes, this is Mary. At least, I think so.'

Dr Patel had heard that before, too. Once he had been annoyed by the jokes and the evasive small talk, but now he understood the despair that lay beneath. His room was a little larger than Joanna's, but it had the same, standard-issue furniture. They sat round the table. Dr Patel opened his laptop. 'Are you comfortable,' he asked.

Not particularly, thought Mary, while Arthur was transported back to childhood lunchtimes and 'Listen with Mother' on the BBC Home Service: 'Are you sitting comfortably? Then I'll begin …' He had soon grown out of the programme, but for a few months he had listened with his mother. 'Yes, thank you,' said Mary and Arthur, almost in unison.

'I'm afraid the news is not very good.' Dr Patel was well practised at this. At the Memory Clinic, the news was rarely very good. 'I've read the report from your doctor and looked at the test Joanna administered in August.' He looked directly at Arthur. 'I fear, Mr Bright, that you are almost certainly in the early stages of dementia. But I'm sure you suspected that already.' Arthur and Mary listened to the oppressive silence. On the road outside, a motorcycle passed noisily. Arthur knew his Latin. 'Demented' meant insane. He imagined the poor lunatics raving in Bedlam and shuddered. A holiday spectacle for the paying public: Roll up, roll up, to see the madmen. 'I've also looked at your MRI scan,' continued Dr Patel smoothly, though he had already left his audience behind. 'There's no sign of any tumour, thank goodness, nor indeed of any vascular dementia. And there's no shrinkage of the frontal lobes which would point towards frontotemporal dementia. That can be a horrible thing, so with luck you've avoided it. But there is a little shrinkage in the temporal lobes, so I think the most likely diagnosis we can make is Alzheimer's disease. I'm very sorry for you both, but it could be worse.'

There was silence again. Most of what Dr Patel had tried to explain had passed them by. Arthur looked both brave and dejected. 'What I don't understand,' he said, 'is why I can still remember things ... from a very long time ago, but yesterday and even ... this morning are already a ... blur. I mean, I don't even know what I had ... for breakfast.'

'It is a bit peculiar, isn't it? It's the way our brains store things. We call it "the dementia bookcase".' Dr Patel pointed to a tall bookcase full of medical tomes. 'You see, the earliest memories are like the books on the lowest shelf and as we go through life we stack them further and further up until the bookcase is almost full. Then our friend Alzheimer's comes along and starts shaking it, only slightly at first and then more and more vigorously. As you'd expect, the top ones fall out first, but however hard it tries, the disease finds it very difficult to dislodge the ones at the bottom. So those early memories are the ones it just can't get at and they're the ones we can stop it stealing. For a time, anyway.'

'I see,' said Arthur slowly, although he was not sure that he did see. Then, with an uncharacteristic outburst, 'Some friend! It's a bastard, this ... Alzheimer's.'

'So what's the prognosis, Doctor?' asked Mary, who had been listening quietly. 'Can you tell us what the future's going to look like?'

Dr Patel paused. 'I'm afraid it's hard to say, Mrs Bright. The disease affects people in so many different ways. Sometimes it develops very slowly and things will carry on much as they are now, but sometimes, if you're unlucky, it can progress quite quickly. I'm sorry I can't be more helpful, but at this stage there is just no telling.'

'And there's nothing at all we can do about it?' There were both anger and fear in Mary's voice.

'Oh yes, there are a few things we can do,' said Dr Patel. He was beaming again. 'We can't cure Alzheimer's yet, but we can try to slow it down and, although it's not easy, it's possible to embrace it and learn to live with it quite well. We sometimes call it the "dementia adventure". It's like Alice going down the rabbit hole and discovering a new and very curious world.' Not surprisingly, neither Arthur nor Mary was in the mood for adventures or rabbit holes. 'I'll prescribe you Donepezil, which can keep the disease in check for a little while, and you should come along to our Memory Café where you can meet others in the same boat. It's held here at the Clinic on the first Tuesday of every month. Coffee and chat, and some excellent cakes. It's all rather jolly. And Joanna is on hand if you have any worries. Someone will contact you in the next few days with the details.'

Arthur imagined Bedlam again. He would prefer to drown than be stuck in a boat with demented people, however jolly they were. He will give the Memory Café a wide berth, thank you very much. 'That sounds like a good idea', he said. 'I'll look forward to it.'

'Let me give you one other piece of advice,' said Dr Patel before he ushered them out. 'Don't let anyone tell you what you can't do. Instead, concentrate on all the things you can do and, as your Mr Churchill used to say, "Keep buggering on".' Such were the demands on the Clinic, it was the last time they would see or hear from Dr Patel. They nodded sympathetically to another couple, much older than them, sitting uncomfortably and anxiously awaiting their turn.

'I'm not sure … we found out anything … new,' said Arthur on the way home, 'and I'm not sure what the bookcase was all about.' Later, Mary would phone Flo and Maria: the news came as no surprise to them. Then she would phone Norman. 'I don't know why I'm phoning you, Norman. There's nothing you can do. There's nothing anyone can do. I'm just feeling so lonely. I wish you were here.'

VI

Lockdown

Donepezil was not a magic cure. It gave Arthur headaches and most likely had something to do with his vivid and unsettling nightmares. It could not stop the disease from tightening its grip, and although with luck it would hold up its advance, time suddenly became more valuable to Arthur and Mary – something to be used before it was taken from them. Typically, Mary was determined to fill however many years – or months – they had left with things they could do together.

Straight away, she took Arthur to the travel agency near Norwich market and they booked a holiday in Malta, where Arthur had always wanted to visit the haunts of the Knights Templar and Hospitaller. A fortnight later they managed to negotiate the airport's snaking queues without too much trouble, although Arthur hated the noise, and he was confused by the machine that scanned his passport and had to be rescued. They stayed at a hotel which overlooked the Grand Harbour in Valetta and, when they were not exploring, Mary swam in the pool and sunbathed while Arthur watched the coming and going of the cruise ships, and the scurrying harbour launches, and the traditional gulets, packed with tourists, which sailed along the coast. Sometimes he picked up his book and started to read, but these days he found it difficult to follow the plot and had to keep looking back to the previous page, and the next day he had forgotten what it was about altogether and had to begin all over again. Each evening they left the hotel to seek out one of the side-street restaurants which catered mainly for locals. They would sit outside, sip their wine, and watch the people who passed by. It did not matter that they quickly ran out of conversation.

There was only one embarrassing incident on the Malta holiday, which would be embroidered further at each telling and become part of family legend. It happened after breakfast one morning when Arthur stepped out of the lift on the wrong floor and was surprised when the key would not open the door of their room. 'Mary,' he shouted, 'Can you let me in?', and, ignoring the 'Do not Disturb' notice, shook the handle insistently. Before long, the door was opened by a man wearing no more than a beard and a bathrobe. 'Yes,' he said angrily. 'Can't you read the notice?'

From behind him came a languid female voice. 'Just send them away, darling, and come back to bed.'

'I do apologise,' said Arthur. 'I seem to have found the wrong room. I hope you're having a nice time,' and he considered it unnecessarily rude when the door was shut firmly in his face. He looked at the key: number 318. He looked at the door: number 218. 'Anyone could make that mistake,' he complained to Mary when eventually he found her on the hotel terrace and recounted his escapade. 'There was no need for him to be so cross.'

'Oh, Arthur!' Mary was unable to contain her laughter. 'The scrapes you get yourself into.'

'We must do this again one day,' said Arthur as at the end of the week they climbed onto the coach which would take them to the airport for the flight home. 'I like it here.' It seemed to Mary that her heart stopped for a moment. She had no idea what the future would hold. She doubted they would return.

Earlier in the year, Arthur had received an invitation from the North Walsham History Society to speak at its December meeting. They had much enjoyed his illuminating talk two years ago on St Benet's Abbey and would he be able to address them on the rise and fall of the North Walsham and Dilham Canal? Arthur had always enjoyed such occasions and had been delighted to accept, but now he was not so sure. 'I really don't know if I can manage it, Mary,' he said.

'Of course you can. It's too good an opportunity to miss and they're relying on you. And they won't be able to find someone else at this stage. As long as you have lots of PowerPoint slides and plenty of notes, you'll be fine. And I'll come with you to cheer you on.'

Arthur forbade the cheering but was easily persuaded. He had a wealth of interesting material on the canal and he was soon engrossed in preparations. There were days when he began to worry it would be a disaster and he considered pleading illness and pulling out, but Mary was having none of it. She reassured him and jollied him along. Until now, he had never seen the need to practise for these events, but this time he had to make sure there would be no hitches and twice Mary was enlisted to watch and listen. 'It's brilliant, Arthur. You haven't lost your touch.' She was not going to mention that he sounded more tentative than she had expected – and with an audience in front of him he was bound to rise to the occasion.

The day arrived. Arthur had emailed his slides in advance, but he packed his laptop as a back-up. He had his file of notes and he gave Mary a second copy 'just in case'; there was also a box of his books – with luck, he might sell a few afterwards. Mary volunteered to drive – since the roadworks incident, Arthur had become nervous of driving at night – and they set off early, finding the church hall venue in good time. In fact, they were the first to arrive. 'You know, I'm quite looking forward to this,' said Arthur and, while they waited, he browsed through his notes yet again. 'I hope we've got the right evening.'

It was the right evening. Before long, the chairman arrived – pompous, but pleasant enough – and, after an over-enthusiastic greeting, Arthur set up his presentation and ran through the first few slides to check he had everything in order. Slowly the hall began to fill – Arthur was, after all, well known to local historians – and before long the chairman was introducing him. 'I'm sure today's speaker, Arthur Bright, needs little introduction. Indeed, many of you will remember Arthur's inspiring account of St Benet's Abbey and you will doubtless have read his fascinating books on Norfolk's history. If you haven't, you might want to buy one or two later. We are so grateful to you, Arthur, for returning to the North Walsham History Society this evening to shed more light on our local canal.'

There was polite applause. Arthur began his talk. Those who knew him well would have noticed an unusual hesitancy and a more frequent reading of his notes, but his old skill had not deserted him and the audience was captivated by his stories that brought the disused waterway back to life. Then – and Arthur never knew how it happened – his sleeve must have brushed against his notes and they fell, scattering onto the floor. There was a time when Arthur would have made light of it and carried on, but now he stumbled and stopped, and bent down to retrieve them. People stirred uneasily. 'I'm so very sorry,' he muttered. 'You'd better talk among yourselves for a moment while I sort myself out.' Mary, who thought it was all her fault for persuading Arthur to come, stood up from the front row to help him. The papers were quickly retrieved, but they were mixed up and unnumbered, and it took some minutes to put them back in the right order. 'Ladies and gentlemen, I do … apologise, but shall we get back to our … cruise along the … canal?' The talking subsided and Arthur tried to pick up the threads he had lost, but his confidence had gone. He looked down and away. He wished he wasn't here. The chairman whispered to Mary. What had happened? Was Arthur ill? Should he rescue him from what had become an embarrassing ordeal for everyone?

'Leave it to me,' said Mary, but just as she was about to intervene, with no idea what she would say, Arthur was taking matters into his own hands.

He took a deep breath and looked directly into the hall. People strained to hear. 'I really am very sorry for ... this unseemly ... performance,' he said. 'I shouldn't have accepted your ... very kind invitation. You see, not that long ago I was diagnosed with ... Alzheimer's, which is a nasty thing and I've tried not to ... admit it, even to myself ... and I thought I could manage. ... But when I'm knocked ... off course I'm clearly all over the place.' He paused again and the silence in the hall was palpable. 'But I don't want to let you ... down, and with your permission, Mr Chairman, I'd like to ... carry on and we'll see how it goes.'

There was a burst of applause and its warmth lifted Arthur's spirits. 'Of course, Arthur, we'd love you to go on.'

Arthur took a sip of water, gathered his notes more neatly and brought up the next slide. For a few minutes he continued to speak quietly and the audience found it difficult to hear, but soon he was back into some sort of stride. Finally, 'So there you have it,' he said. I doubt the canal will ever be properly navigable again, but all power to the ... volunteers for their efforts. And I do apologise again to you all for not being at my best ... this evening.'

The clapping began immediately, rose to a crescendo, and carried on and on. When at last it died down, the chairman was on his feet. 'Thank you so much, Arthur. I don't quite know how to follow that. I know everyone will agree that not only have we learnt much that we never knew about our canal, but we have also witnessed a most remarkable act of bravery.' He was relieved the talk had been rescued and he might even have meant what he said. 'I think we might let Arthur off the hook and forego the usual questions, so shall we go straight to our customary Christmas refreshments to round off the evening? And don't forget there are some of Arthur's books on sale.'

And so the evening went on, with sherry and mince pies, lively chatter, and everyone wanting to offer Arthur their congratulations, and Mary sold many more books than she had expected, which

I Am Arthur Bright

Arthur was happy to sign. Then Mary saw that he was tiring, and they collected their things and slipped quietly away.

'What a performance, Arthur!' said Mary when they were safely back in the car. 'I was so proud of you. And you sold dozens of books! We ought to go for a drink ... and why not sausage and chips?'

'That would be ... nice. ... At the King's Head? That went ... rather well, didn't it?' The dropped notes were no longer a concern. 'I suppose I am quite ... hungry.' So sausage and chips it was – at the first pub they came to.

The following week a letter arrived from North Walsham, thanking Arthur for his fascinating address, wishing him well, and hoping he would speak to them again. For some reason they never got round to contacting him.

*

As Christmas approached, there was the usual round of drinks parties – at the Maddermarket, at the Historical Society, with Mary's antiques colleagues, and with neighbours and friends. Arthur no longer enjoyed such gatherings. He felt awkward; he found it more and more difficult to follow conversations and, because he kept making the same comment or asking the same question, he found people he did not know would excuse themselves more-or-less politely and move away. Mary, however, was adamant that socialising was good for him and would not allow him to escape.

At Christmas, the family gathered at Rose Bank, where Maria and family stayed for three days and Flo's tribe drove down on Christmas Day. The twins had both offered to act as host to give Mary a rest, but she was adamant that Arthur would be happier in his own home. With Arthur's help, she decorated the house and put up a large Christmas tree. Two days before Christmas, Arthur and Mary went to the Cathedral in Norwich, as they always did, for the traditional carol service. Arthur was enchanted by it all and joined in loudly with the congregational carols, and Mary prayed silently that his dementia would not progress too quickly, although she had never quite believed and was sure her prayer would go unanswered. On Christmas Eve, with Maria's family, they went to midnight mass at St Andrew's church and saw so many people they knew who wished them 'Happy Christmas'. By now, they had heard of Arthur's troubles, but they did not patronise him, and did not mind he had forgotten their names and said the same thing again and again. And again. On Christmas Day itself, they sat around the tree and exchanged presents (none of which was a surprise, although they pretended it was), and Mary had prepared a sumptuous lunch, and Arthur did not follow the conversations but just liked being in the middle of them. They drew the curtains, and the pudding flamed with brandy, and the sprig of holly crackled, and they all made their secret wishes. In the afternoon, after a brisk walk by the river, they played board games, and John, who was especially good with his grandad, played alongside him. Then they played charades, and there was much hilarity, and Arthur, who had no idea what was going on, chuckled happily and had another glass of sherry.

'I'm shattered,' said Mary that night, when the washing-up had been done and Flo and family had left. 'But I think they all had a good time, don't you?'

'I'm sure they did,' said Arthur. 'Thank you for a ... wonderful day, Mary. You excelled yourself. ... That John's a nice boy, isn't he?'

'Yes, but they're all nice. We should be very proud of them.'

'And they should be ... very proud of you. It was the best Christmas ever.' Arthur could still remember his mother's last Christmas which he had spoiled; he could remember the twins' first magical Christmas at The Moorings; and, more hazily, he could remember the Christmas on *Still Waters*, which they had decorated with fairy lights, and Mary's parents had slept without complaining on the sofa bed, and they had lit candles and sung carols while Mary played her guitar. But this one outdid them all.

Next morning, Maria's family had all begun their breakfast when Arthur appeared in his dressing gown. 'Happy Christmas everybody!'

'Christmas was yesterday, Grandad,' said John.

'Was it? … Now you say it, I do … remember … vaguely. Anyway, I don't see why … we can't have another Christmas today. What do you think?'

'Good idea, Grandad!'

'So will you be doing the cooking, John?' asked Mary, smiling.

*

That afternoon, Maria and family departed and Rose Bank felt strangely empty. Mary was tired but she missed the company and was worried what the coming year would bring. She would take it a day at a time and she hoped Arthur would not deteriorate too much. At the beginning of January, after the New Year crowds had left, she and Arthur drove to the beach at Horsey to see the seals and their pups, as they had always done at this time of year since the children were young. They never grew tired of watching the extraordinary creatures which spent half their lives at sea, feeding on fish and building up their reserves of blubber, and the other half on land, mating, breeding and moulting. The older, spotted grey seals lay still, or gossiped, or argued, or flapped their way clumsily across the sand, not quite at home out of the water. The white pups were more lively. Five weeks after they had been born, they would be abandoned by their mothers and launch themselves into the waves to make their own way in the watery world. In the autumn, by some instinct, they would return, and the cycle would begin again.

For more than an hour, Arthur and Mary sat on the concrete walkway which separated the beach from the dunes, huddled in their coats and scarves and woolly hats against the cold sea breeze. They smelled the seaweed and listened, mesmerised, to the heaving water.

They shared their binoculars, and pointed out to each other a squabble, or a comic turn, or an uncertain pup deciding whether or not to venture into the unknown. They warmed themselves with hot chocolate from a Thermos flask and ate mince pies left over from Christmas. They talked to the volunteer rangers, some of whom they had come to know, who were themselves drawn to the beach each year when the seals came and took it in turns to protect them from the sightseers and their dogs, and the stone-throwing children, or to disentangle them from the detritus of humans. And as they looked, Arthur was taken back to that other beach, and an image of his dying father; and Mary worried again about the year ahead, and about Arthur, and about herself, although she could share none of this with Arthur and just snuggled closer to him.

*

So 2020 began – for the Chinese, who know about such things, it was the Year of the Rat – and Arthur and Mary settled back into some sort of dull routine. Arthur continued to collect his morning paper from Mr Shastri, but he was more careful. He had, with some difficulty, learned how to use his mobile phone and Mary had put a tracker on it and made sure he carried his address with him. On Mondays they would have lunch at the pub – a special deal for 'senior citizens'; on Tuesdays, Mary would rehearse at the Maddermarket (Arthur was under strict instruction not to leave the house); on Wednesdays they would shop at the supermarket; and on Fridays they would take the bus into Norwich, and buy fruit and vegetables in the market, and browse in the medieval streets, and have lunch in Jarrolds or the Assembly Rooms. They no longer went to Bridge Club – Arthur could not remember who had played what card – and Arthur even missed meetings of the Historical Society, which hitherto had been the highlight of his month. Without telling him, Mary closed her shop and put the business up for sale. At Rose Bank, while Arthur pottered in his book-filled study and made no headway with his long-planned history of Thorpe St Andrew, Mary set up her easel and resurrected her neglected painting skills. She found the winter almost unbearably dull and yearned for the coming of spring, when they could enjoy the garden and go out walking, and she would book them another holiday as well. At the beginning of February, Norman came to stay, which for different reasons was a diversion and a comfort to them both.

But even this dull routine was soon to change into something far worse. The headlines warned of a new and insidious virus circulating in China and spreading across the world. It might have started with bats, or in the animal markets, or leaking from a laboratory, but that did not matter. What mattered was that by March it was creeping into the United Kingdom and people were dying. Pubs, restaurants, cinemas, schools, sporting events and non-essential shops were closed, and there was a legally enforceable instruction to 'stay at home'. Every day, if the weather allowed, Arthur and Mary went for a walk together – the single exercise allowed under the law – but since it was the elderly who were most at risk, and Flo and Maria made them promise not to go out shopping, they were otherwise confined to Rose Bank. Their neighbours, the Watsons, were good enough to leave a newspaper from Shastri's every day, and sometimes bread and milk, but they would not come close; otherwise Mary ordered her groceries online and they were delivered to the door. 'We shouldn't complain,' said Mary. 'We're lucky to have a garden and not a flat in a high-rise block, and we don't have to worry about jobs or housebound children.' She continued with her artistic endeavours, persuaded Arthur to play Scrabble (though he had lost his old skill and no longer understood the scoring), and unearthed some of the twins' jigsaws from long ago which they enjoyed doing together. On Thursday evenings, like most others in the village, they stood outside and 'clapped for carers' – a sign of appreciation for the overrun health professionals who worked unstintingly on the front line. Nevertheless, Mary felt trapped in the house with poor Arthur, without the respite of family and friends. There would not be a spring holiday after all, the play she was rehearsing at the Maddermarket had been cancelled, and there was no knowing how long the restrictions would last. When she watched on television the carefully managed press conferences from Downing Street, she did not believe a single bombastic word the politicians uttered. Arthur, on the other hand, found the whole Covid business quite liberating: Mary could not drag him to the shops and now there would be none of the socialising which he found so uncomfortable. He could muddle along quite happily and stop trying to make up excuses.

In May, the lockdown restrictions were gradually eased, but the virus had not gone away and Arthur and Mary, like most people of their age, continued to take care. They donned their face masks, sanitised their hands, and went to Mr Shastri's when they knew it would not be busy. In June, when the weather was warm enough, they thought it would be safe to invite Flo and family for a barbecue – as long as they all stayed outside and kept their distance. Mary felt they had to get away: a foreign holiday was out of the question and she felt nervous about hotels, so in July she booked a motor cruiser on the Broads – something she and Arthur had not done since the children left home. Warnes' yard had long since closed, so they picked up a cruiser in Wroxham, a few miles north of Norwich on the banks of the River Bure. The town was alive with excited holidaymakers, and there were boats everywhere, setting off from the boatyards or waiting to go through the bridge; and husbands and wives were arguing, children were shouting and cheering, tee-shirted teenagers were lolling on deck with their radios blaring, and one boat had run into another. 'Hullaballoos, the lot of them,' muttered Arthur, who on Mary's insistence had taken the wheel and was steering calmly through the melee. Although he was forgetting most things, his nautical skill had not been impaired.

On their first evening afloat, they were fortunate enough to find a mooring alongside the Green at Horning, where the Swan Inn stands on the sharp turn in the river, and Southgates' shed has the bustling Main Street on one side and the water lapping on the other, and the one-design sailing boats race each other along the 'Reach'. As the week went on, they spent a night at Ranworth, climbed the church tower and looked out over the watery countryside; they wended their slow way up the narrow River Ant, which opens onto the expanse of Barton Broad, and moored on the tiny staithe at Neatishead, with supper at the White Horse inn. Back on the River Bure, they tied up next to the ruins of St Benet's Abbey, which Arthur wanted to visit again, and then turned onto the River Thurne, passed picturesque Thurne Mill, and moored at Potter Heigham, whose ancient bridge was the gateway to their most treasured places, Hickling Broad and Horsey Mere, from where you can walk across the marsh to the sea. But their time was running out, and they had to turn and hurry back to Wroxham and to home. At Rose Bank, Arthur thanked Mary for their voyage down 'memory lane'. On the water, he had felt quite his old self, but the following day he had very little memory of it at all.

*

At Marsh View, as evening falls and Alice comes in to close the curtains, Arthur is looking at the photographs of that summer in his book. One is 'On Barton Broad', and Arthur is steering. 'Quite the Admiral, aren't you?' says Alice admiringly.

'Did you know that … Nelson learned to sail on … Barton Broad? I always used to tell my … classes that when we studied the Battle of … Trafalgar.'

The other photograph, taken at Rose Bank that same summer, is 'In the Rose Garden'. Arthur and Mary are sitting together in the garden, apparently unaware of the camera and perfectly content. The garden looks overgrown, with weeds and nettles among the flowers, but, as he looks, Arthur can almost smell the heady fragrance of the roses. They say scent is the last sense that Alzheimer's can destroy.

'Who's that ... old lady ... next to me?' asks Arthur, puzzled.

'It's Mary, of course.'

'No. ... Are you sure? ... Mary was ... much younger than that. ... I wonder what ... happened to her.'

*

The easing of the Covid 'Stay at Home' restrictions over the summer turned out to be only temporary. New variants of the virus meant infections and deaths began to rise exponentially, and by November the country was in a second lockdown. Mary had clung to Dr Patel's advice to fight dementia by 'buggering on', but buggering on had become impossible and, with winter weather closing in again, they were once more trapped at Rose Bank. She was unsure whether Arthur's condition was deteriorating faster or whether she was finding it harder to cope with his confusions. On bad days she found herself becoming impatient and irate, and was almost immediately consumed by remorse. When Christmas came round again, the restrictions were eased for a few days, but despite her longing for other company she decided it would be too risky to meet with the family. So she put up a few half-hearted festive decorations, cooked a turkey crown and a shop-bought Christmas pudding, and opened a bottle of wine. She turned on the television to watch the Queen's speech, Arthur fell asleep and snored, and she drank a generous loyal toast alone. She just hoped the new vaccinations would set them free before too long. 'I know it's been a bit quiet today,' said Arthur later, 'but it's been rather nice with just the two of us, hasn't it?'

'I'm glad you've enjoyed it,' said Mary, wishing it had not been just the two of them. She had not enjoyed it at all.

After a supper of left-overs, Mary phoned Flo, then Maria. She wanted to wish them and their families a Happy Christmas, but more than that she wanted to talk to someone different. 'I think Mum sounded seriously fed up,' said Flo to David when she had put the phone down. 'She tried to hide it, but it wasn't like her at all.'

'It must be a never-ending nightmare, looking after your dad. The dementia is bad enough for her to live with, without all this isolation, but I don't see there's much we can do.'

'I must try to speak to her more often. So must Maria. I don't know how much longer Mum can cope.'

At Rose Bank, Arthur looked up from an old newspaper. 'I hope my mother is … all right. Perhaps I … should phone her too, or we could both … go to see her … tomorrow.'

Mary groaned inside. Arthur's long-dead mother was becoming an insoluble problem. 'We're not allowed to meet people because of the Covid. That's why we've been on our own. But next week we could go to look at the seals, like we always do'.

'Mm that's a … good idea,' said Arthur. 'We could do with … going out again. … And we must go … to see my mother.'

*

Eventually the frosts and snow flurries gave way to March winds and April showers, and outside, in the neglected garden of Rose Bank, the snowdrops gave way to crocuses, daffodils and primroses, which in turn gave way to tulips and bluebells. Inside, however, Arthur's decline continued, speeded by the isolation imposed by the pandemic. He became more forgetful and confused, and consequently became unreasonably stubborn as he fought to retain his independence. He had always been the mildest and most accepting of men, but now he could be querulous and even aggressive when a once simple task proved beyond him. Just as he found it impossible to follow the plot of a novel or story, in the same way he lost interest in television, unless the programme was singing and dancing, or wildlife films; speech was more difficult for him and he was less steady on his feet. Although he could not cope with large numbers of people, what he missed most was the lack of human contact: the daily chats with Mr Shastri, neighbours dropping in, friendly faces in the street, even the schoolchildren staring at their phones. Only in listening to music did he find some solace. Mary, who was also lonely and unsupported, bore the brunt of Arthur's frustrations. On one level his outbursts made her resentful and short-tempered – she was doing her best but she was suffering with him; on another level she understood his despair and wanted only to look after him; and in doing so, strangely perhaps, she felt closer to him than she had done since their student years.

Slowly, with the ramped-up delivery of vaccines, Covid lost its stranglehold on the country and one by one, reluctantly masked, the population emerged into the sunlight of a world perceptibly changed. Arthur and Mary emerged with them. Now Mary always walked with Arthur to buy the newspaper and she sat with him by the river or for a drink in the pub garden: they were prisoner and escort, although no-one could be sure which was which. However, they continued to avoid supermarkets and crowded places, which suited Arthur with his aversion to hustle and bustle and noise. Turn by turn, Flo and Maria came to visit: as much as possible they kept their distance, but it was a relief for Mary, tired and dark-eyed, to unload the problems she was having with Dad. 'You can't go on like this,' they said. 'You must get some help.' But it wasn't that easy: Arthur didn't want help, even from Mary.

Mr and Mrs Watson from next door continued to be good Samaritans. They would come in for tea one afternoon each week or invite Arthur and Mary to theirs. Arthur enjoyed the company and Mary welcomed the respite. In due course, it was arranged for one of them to sit with Arthur for an evening each week, so Mary could return to the Maddermarket and take a very small part in its next production. Norman was another Samaritan: he visited more often, stayed over, and was immensely patient. He talked to Arthur about their childhood in Hartbourne, which Arthur could just about remember (and, yes, he did remember the school, and Mrs Jones, and, quite clearly, Sarah) and enjoyed the reminiscences. And when Arthur had retired to bed and was asleep, Norman would comfort Mary. 'Just hold me tonight, Norman,' she said one evening. I don't have the energy for anything else. And I can't anymore, while Arthur's upstairs. Not here. Not now.' She looked away. 'You mean so much to me, Norman, but I can't forgive myself for the way I've cheated on Arthur. He never deserved it.' And uncontrollable sobs welled up from deep inside her. Her life was becoming unbearable.

For a few days in August, Arthur and Mary stayed with Flo in Sheringham, and although Arthur was unsettled away from Rose Bank, the days spent revisiting the coast and looking out over the marshes gave him immense pleasure. On one very special day, they drove to the University of Norfolk where they had first met all those years ago, and although the temporary buildings had broken their anchor chains and drifted away, and so much more had been built, there was much that had stayed the same and even for Arthur there were moments when a happy flicker of recognition lit up his ageing face. At the end of the month, while the weather held, Mary hired a day boat for them from the yard at Potter Heigham, and Arthur steered through the narrow bridge, and they ventured out onto Hickling Broad. They watched the sailing dinghies tacking from shore to shore and found a quiet mooring for their picnic lunch, and then Arthur became restless and insisted they go back because his mother would be worrying. Mary took a photograph of Arthur at the University and another of him enjoying his picnic afloat. They would one day be the last two photographs in his *Story*. It was just a shame that while Mary would treasure these times, although (as it turned out) not for long, for Arthur every experience was fleeting and forgotten as soon as it was done.

There were also more incidents, like the one in the hotel in Malta, which could be relied on to provoke well-meaning laughter (although probably not when they occurred) and would add further to the store of Arthurian legend. The first was the matter of the pie. Before Alzheimer's arrived, Arthur had been a competent cook, but now the simplest processes eluded him. He could just about manage boiling the kettle and making a hot drink, but even that had become a struggle. So one day, when Mary had to go out for a couple of hours, she left him a chicken and mushroom pie for his lunch with a clearly written instruction: 'Heat the oven to 180 deg. and put in the pie for 20 minutes'. 'I can manage that,' said Arthur testily. 'I'm not stupid. You go and enjoy yourself.' At lunchtime, Arthur did as he was told. He switched on the oven, turned the dial to '180' and, when the red light went out, put in the pie. After twenty minutes, he opened the oven and was alarmed by the black smoke that poured out. The pie was charred on the top and covered in ash. He didn't fancy eating it.

'Was the pie all right?' asked Mary, when she returned.

Arthur was sheepish. 'I'm afraid it got … burnt.'

'Oh, Arthur. How did you forget it?'

'I didn't. I did just … as you told me.'

Mary surveyed the remains. 'But Arthur, you didn't take it out of the wrapping!'

'How was I … to know?' protested Arthur. 'You didn't say … anything about that.'

Another and more disastrous incident was the Rose Bank flood. Although Arthur found it more and more difficult, he refused to let Mary help him with washing and dressing, and that morning he was running himself a bath while she was in the garden taking the deadheads from the late-flowering roses. The telephone rang and Arthur thought he had better go down to the hall and answer it. It was Maria wanting to speak to Mum, but Arthur enjoyed chatting to her about the grandchildren, then went to the door and called Mary. 'Phone ... for you, dear. It's ... Maria.' Mary took her time, but as soon as she stepped inside she could not miss the damp patch which was spreading across the ceiling and the water dripping from the light fitting. There was a rivulet trickling down the stairs. From a hundred miles away, Maria heard the calamity unfolding. 'Arthur! The bath! You've left the taps running.' Footsteps thundering up the stairs. 'Just stay there, Arthur. Tell Maria I'll call her back later.'

'Oh dear. I must've ... forgotten.' Then a dull thud and, 'It's the ... ceiling ... Mary.' A pause and more footsteps. 'Mum says ... she'll call you ... later. ... No ... here she is. It's been ... nice ... talking to you. I hope we'll ... see you ... soon.'

Mary took the receiver. 'Maria ...'

'Mum, are you all right?'

'No, I'm bloody well not all right. There's water everywhere, and plaster, and ... I just can't do this, Maria.' And she burst into uncharacteristic tears.

'Oh Mum. It all sounds dreadful. Have a cup of tea and then clear up what you can. I'm going to come over. And I'll phone Flo. I'll be there about lunchtime.'

'No, there's no need. I was just being stupid. I'm OK now. I was just having a moment. It's only water, after all. I'm sure I can cope.'

'I'm sure you can, Mum, but I'm coming over anyway. See you soon.' And she hung up before Mary could protest further.

Mary took a deep breath. She was pleased Maria was coming and she knew she couldn't go on coping. 'Come on Arthur, you silly billy, go and get dressed. I'll put the kettle on and we can see about clearing up later. Maria's driving over to help us.'

'That'll be nice,' said Arthur as he stood in the midst of the chaos. 'We haven't ... seen her for ... some time.'

*

Looking back, after the carpets had dried and the builder had repaired the ceiling, the flood did have its comic side, but it was also the event which caused Flo and Maria to insist Mary took on more permanent help; and although Mary was reluctant at first, she agreed it was worth a try. Not only was she exhausted, but it had become clear to her that her relationship with Arthur had changed again. Alzheimer's may, in one way, have drawn them closer together, but instead of being husband and wife, they had morphed into patient and carer. They no longer talked to each other as they used to talk, nor relaxed in and enjoyed each other's company. Rather, as the disease tightened its grip on Arthur, Mary had become variously nurse, valet, cleaner, cook, driver and protector, and everything that really mattered was being squeezed out. She was eternally grateful to the Watsons for allowing her to escape for two or three hours each week, but after the flood it came to her with utter clarity that what she wanted and needed even more than escape was a little time each day to be with Arthur, and to love him as she used to love him, and to shut out the endless dependence and drudgery that was coming between them. She was quite sure, although Arthur could not express it, that he had retained enough emotional intelligence to feel the same. Thus, after much searching, young and happy-go-lucky Mrs Carberry, with her peaches and cream complexion and soft Irish lilt, arrived at Rose Bank, sometimes in the morning and sometimes in the afternoon. She was willing to turn her hand to most things and was not a busybody, and Arthur found her to be a friend, not a threat, and it seemed the flood had been an unexpected blessing.

Yet the disease was not to be thwarted that easily. Arthur's nightmares grew more terrifying and he began to suffer from night-time incontinence. He raged at the indignity of incontinence pads. They were nappies that made him a baby again and he would hurl them across the room. Worse, his behaviour towards Mary could be disturbingly aggressive and she telephoned the Memory Clinic for advice. Dr Patel was not available, but someone would get back to her and eventually it was decided to discontinue the Donepezil which had done its job as much as it could and might now be contributing to Arthur's problems. As a result, the nightmares gradually lost their cruel power, but the outbursts of aggression remained. At first, it appeared they were a symptom of Arthur's struggle to retain some sort of independence, but by the spring of 2022 there were moments when he did not recognize Mary. On some evenings he insisted she was not his wife and refused to let her into the bedroom; too often he thought she was an intruder and once he threatened her with a knife from the kitchen; and in the garden, especially if they had had an inconsequential argument, he would catch her trying to steal the flowers and would chase her with a garden fork or a pair of shears. On these occasions, she would retreat to the Watsons next door: Mr Watson would go round to placate Arthur, who greeted him with genuine courtesy and wondered what the fuss was about. Mary knew all this was the disease and not Arthur, but she was frightened. She made an appointment to see Dr Thomas. Predictably his computer was no help and he could offer nothing except sympathy. Such behaviour, he said, was not uncommon in the later stages of Alzheimer's. She must try to stay calm and talk gently to Arthur. Perhaps she could put on some calming music. Above all, she must try to stay safe herself and use 111 or 999 to summon help if necessary. Mary found it all well-meaning but quite unrealistic.

One day, towards the end of March, the crisis towards which all these miserable events had been moving finally occurred. Mary did not know what it was that sparked Arthur's foul outburst, but she could take no more. Luckily Mrs Carberry was on hand to calm him with her Irish charm. 'Oh yes, Arthur, you're all sweetness and light to her, but you treat me like dirt,' shouted Mary, and instantly regretted it. There must have been a trigger that Arthur could not or would not explain.

'I think you're in need of a break, Mrs Bright,' said Mrs Carberry later. She was not being critical. She could see that Mary's abundance of good sense and love was running dry.

Mary swallowed hard. 'You're right, Mrs Carberry. Arthur doesn't mean to behave like that and the way I spoke to him was unforgiveable. But I just couldn't help it.'

'No-one could look after Mr Bright better than you,' said Mrs Carberry. 'I don't know anyone else with so much patience. But you need to go off and recharge your batteries or you'll be ill yourself, don't you see? I'd be quite happy to stay over and look after Mr Bright for a couple of days so you can get a well-earned rest.'

'Would you really, Mrs Carberry?' Until now, it had not crossed Mary's mind, but it was exactly what she wanted to hear. She knew she could not go on. 'It would do me good and it would be good for Arthur, too.' Mrs Carberry was an absolute treasure.

And so it was arranged. On the following day, after lunch, Mary would drive up to Sheringham and stay with Flo, and Mrs Carberry would sleep in the spare room at Rose Bank. Arthur was a bit muddled but considered it a splendid idea. 'You go and ... enjoy yourself ... Mary. You deserve a ... holiday and I'll be quite ... all right with Mrs ... Cadbury.'

Before she set off, Mary hugged him tightly. It was the first time they would be apart since before the pandemic and, in spite of everything, she would miss him hugely. 'You're going to have a lovely time as well, Arthur. Lots of chocolate, I expect. Make sure you behave yourself – and look after Mrs Carberry until I get back.' She kissed him lightly on his still unshaven cheek and turned quickly away.

*

Mary was not expected at Flo's until later, so she had planned to make another visit to the seals at Horsey on the way. The pups would have left, but the adults would still be scratching out their old coats on the sand. The road took her across the bridge at Acle, and through Martham and Fleggburgh. There was always something eerie about the sweep of wetlands where the derelict wind pumps, which had once drained the marshes, were silhouetted against the wide horizon. At Horsey, even before she parked, she could hear the waves gathering their strength before tumbling onto the sand and she could smell the salty tang of the sea. In fact, she realised it was as much the sea as the seals that had brought her here: ever since her walks with Arthur in their student days, she had been drawn by its restorative power. She had loved the river at Thorpe, but the sea was different – impersonal, elemental, the home of Neptune and of mermaids. On the beach, she shivered in the biting easterly breeze and noticed the storm clouds which threatened in the distance. She stood for a while and watched the awkward creatures which would soon be leaving for who knows where, but as the rain began to fall she retreated to the sanctuary of the car. She wondered how Arthur was faring with 'Mrs Cadbury', and how she was faring with him. She flicked open her phone, but thank goodness there were no messages. She started the engine. She would follow the coast road as far as Sea Palling, then turn inland to Stalham before heading north to Sheringham. Flat fields spread in all directions, punctuated only by the lonely farmsteads, a few houses, and almost as many isolated churches. Who built the churches, whom did they serve all those years ago, and were they now abandoned and locked up, waiting without hope for worshippers who never came? The rain was falling more heavily and the windscreen wipers were finding it hard to cope. There was a clap of thunder overhead and a fork of lightning, zigzagging down to the black earth, lit up the barren landscape.

As Mary drove, her mind turned to Arthur and how he was being dragged inexorably away from her. She wanted time to stop, so they could stay together for longer, but then he would be caught for longer between sanity and madness, and she would be caught with him. She wanted time to turn back to when they lived on *Still Waters* with all the optimism of their youth, and so many possibilities lay ahead of them, and they had no awareness of how it would all end. Or to turn back further and, knowing what she knew now, would she have married Arthur at all? Of course she would. There may have been regrets, but on balance theirs had been a good life, and they had wonderful children and grandchildren, but now fate was exacting its price. Surely she had no choice other than to go on? Wrapped in such thoughts, and with the rain washing across the windscreen, Mary did not see, or did not want to see, until it was too late, the sharp twist in the road and the ancient, steadfast tree towering in front of her. At the last second, she braked fiercely, but the tyres could find no grip on the standing water. The car slewed through the fence and into the gnarled trunk beyond. A crash, drowned out by the storm, and then silence as the thunder rolled on and away.

It was some minutes before the crumpled car was discovered by another traveller. A bloodied body was slumped over the steering wheel. There was no sign of life. An ambulance and a police car came, their blue lights flashing through the gloom, but there was nothing that could be done. On the back windscreen of Mary's car was the stupid sticker John had given her, transformed into something horribly ironic: 'Please Pass Quietly. Driver Asleep.'

At Flo's house, there was a knock at the door. At Rose Bank, Arthur had enjoyed his afternoon talking with Mrs Carberry. 'Mary should be at Flo's by now,' she said.

'I should ... think so,' said Arthur. 'I hope she didn't get ... caught in all that ... rain. ... We should go ... to see my ... mother ... later.'

VII

Marsh View

Mary's funeral is well attended. Apart from the family, there are the Watsons from next door and so many other friends from the village; Mrs Carberry; beaming Mr Shastri; antiques dealers; members of the Norwich Players; Bill Chalmers and members of the Bridge Club; Jack Warnes from the defunct boatyard; Ray ('I don't think you've met my husband, Arthur?'); Norman, who is visibly upset: a shocked procession from every walk of Mary's life. Arthur is bewildered by it all. He is lost without Mary and is still waiting for her to come home.

Days drag by. At Rose Bank, Arthur picks up the service sheet from the funeral and looks at it, but only casually. He has not taken in what has happened. 'Shall we go for a walk, Dad?' asks Flo. She has stayed with him since the crash happened and tomorrow Maria will come and take over, but it is only a temporary arrangement. Both Flo and Maria have their own families and cannot desert them. Mrs Carberry has agreed to spend more time with Arthur: she will help him get up in the morning and will put him to bed in the evening, but it is only a stopgap and will not be enough. He will need someone with him most of the time. He cannot cook for himself or look after the house and garden. If he is left alone, he will let himself out and go wandering, and more than likely will not find his way home. Flo and Maria are not hard-hearted and have wondered if Arthur could live with one of them, perhaps in a 'grandad' annex, but it would still be difficult to leave him on his own. It would be a huge tie and one that would impact unreasonably on their own lives and the lives of everyone close to them. They have seen the terrible toll Arthur's dementia took on their mother – they are sure the accident was caused by her exhaustion – yet they cannot stop feeling they should do more. They have considered finding a team of live-in carers, but as well as the eye-watering expense, it would not give Arthur the stability he needs.

On the next day, Maria arrives. Before Flo heads back to Sheringham, the three of them walk slowly down to the pub for lunch. There is a chill in the air, but there is a fire blazing and spitting, and they sit at a table by the window overlooking the river and the island. On the island, the once bustling boatyards have gone and there is only a string of raggedy boats moored haphazardly along the bank: cheap foreign holidays have sent the hire industry into decline.

'I wonder what happened to ... *Still Waters*,' says Arthur. Naturally they are all feeling fragile. 'It's a pity ... your mother isn't here. She liked watching ... the river.' Does he remember why she isn't here, the twins ask themselves. Is he expecting her to come back from her shop with all the usual gossip?

Maria broaches the dreadful subject. 'Dad, we've got to decide where you're going to live now Mum's gone.'

'Isn't she ... coming back?'

'No, Dad, she had an accident, didn't she?'

Arthur wrinkles his brow. 'I do remember ... something about it,' he says. 'Poor Mum. ... So she's not coming back?'

'No, Dad.'

'Well, I'm sure ... I'll be all right. You'll be ... staying here, won't you?'

'I'll be here next week, but I can't stay with you for ever,' says Maria. 'Jill and John are already complaining about having to fend for themselves.'

'Jill and John? I don't believe ... I've seen them ... for a long time.'

'You saw them last week at the funeral, Dad.'
'Did I?' says Arthur. 'I've … had a sleep since then.'
'We think it'd be nice if you came to live near one of us,' says Flo. 'So we can visit you more often.'
'You mean move … from here?'
'Well Rose Bank's going to be far too big for one person. You'll get lost in it by yourself.'
'I do … sometimes … get lost,' says Arthur. He is not being serious.
'Maybe some sort of sheltered accommodation,' suggests Maria, 'where there's a manager you can call on if you need to? We could look for somewhere near the sea.' Maria does not mean sheltered accommodation. Arthur needs looking after all the time. But if she suggests a care home, he will dig in his heels and they will have got nowhere.
Flo raises an eyebrow. She lives by the sea, but Maria does not.
'I'm not sure,' says Arthur. 'I'd rather … stay here. I'll think … about it.'
They look at the beer-stained menu without enthusiasm. 'You choose for me,' says Arthur: he can no longer choose for himself. Flo goes to order at the bar. They all need time, but time is something they do not have. Later, before Flo leaves, she and Maria agree to start looking for a suitable care home, wherever it might be. They know Arthur will never willingly accept the idea, but what other option is there? It is an impossible situation. They weep for their Mum, and for Dad, and for themselves. Damn Dr Alzheimer: they have come to personify the disease – it makes it easier to rail against – although it is unfair on the good Doctor who, in the nineteenth century, was the hero who identified pre-senile dementia and not a villain at all. Later that afternoon, Flo climbs into her car, sits for a moment, breathes in deeply. 'Drive carefully,' says Maria, 'and make sure to ring when you get home.'

'I'll be fine,' says Flo. 'Poor Dad. But there's nothing else we can do.' She lets in the clutch and pulls away.

*

Flo and Maria research care homes – near Sheringham, where Flo lives; in the Midlands, where Maria lives; and around Norwich. They talk to friends and are reassured and disturbed in equal measure. They search the web, read idealised brochures, study inspection reports, make phone calls. 'No thank you, we won't make an appointment. We'll get back to you when we're ready.' They are not going to make that mistake; they will turn up unannounced and ask to look round there and then. Flo focuses on homes near Sheringham and in Norwich; Maria does the same for homes near her. If they find a 'possible', they will make a second visit together. When they agree on a 'probable', they will take Arthur. They know he will object strenuously, but they owe him that much. It is a daunting task, and they have to negotiate jobs and families as well, but it is made easier by the 'sniff test'. If at the door they are hit by the stale smell of urine, they need go no further. It is not a characteristic mentioned in the publicity, but it happens too often. How are the staff and residents immune to something so basic and so unpleasant? An overpowering smell of air freshener is nearly as bad. At one establishment – Sundowner – the smell is masked by the alcohol on Matron's breath. It's shocking, thinks Flo, but it's a job that would drive me to drink.

It is a relief, therefore, that at a newly opened care home in Sheringham the air is fresh. It is a modern purpose-built complex and scrupulously clean. Two ladies are going out for a walk: they might be guests at a high-class hotel. There is an almost too effusive welcome from the receptionist, who takes some details. 'Of course, if you can wait a couple of minutes, the manager will show you round.' The staff are smiling and most of the patients are cheerful when Flo talks to them. The corridors are brightly lit and there is artwork on the walls. But Flo wonders if it might all be too clinical, too tidy: Mum and Dad had always lived in a happy clutter. In the dining room they are laying the tables for lunch. The food smells appetising and, she is assured, it is all cooked on the premises. The menu is varied and the sort of traditional fare elderly people would like. If Flo comes back with Maria, she will make sure it is at a mealtime. Some of the residents are in the lounge – talking, reading, sleeping. They are pleased to see her and, yes, they do like it here. Nothing is too much trouble. Some of them are very old and have to be helped in and out of their chairs; they shuffle around with their trolleys and their Zimmer frames. Dad might not like this. He does not think he is old. And, after all, his body is not old; it is just his mind that no longer works as it should.

The manager asks more about Arthur. Yes, they do have a number of residents with dementia. If they have a diagnosis, they live separately on the first floor: we find they can upset the other residents. 'I'll show you.' At the top of the stairs, the manager punches in a code and opens the door. Flo knows it has to be secure or these residents would wander off, but it is like entering a jailhouse. They go into the first-floor lounge. A few people sit around doing nothing; none of them bothers to look up. There is a television, but nobody is watching. Flo is visibly appalled. Dad is not like any of these people. Not yet, anyway. Did they come here like this, or is it what an institution has done to them? 'Of course, there will be a number of activities this afternoon,' says the manager, noticing Flo's dismay.

'What sort of activities?'

'Board games, art, physical exercises. We try to give them as many interesting things to do as we can.'

Flo nods her agreement. Dad wouldn't be interested in any of these. All snakes and no ladders. 'Do you take them out into the garden?'

The manager hesitates. 'Yes, we do, whenever we can spare the staff, but it has to be in very small groups to keep them safe.' It is a glorious spring morning; no-one is in the garden.

'So will they be going down for lunch soon?' asks Flo.

'Our dementia residents have their own dining room up here, but most of them have lunch in their room. Would you like to see?'

They walk along the landing. Through an open door, Flo glimpses a woman lying in a foetal position on her bed; and then another and another. 'I think I've seen enough. Thank you for your time,' she says. Flo has heard how some care homes routinely sedate their most troubled (or troublesome?) residents, apparently for their own good: could that possibly be what is happening here? She can guess where these women will have lunch, if they can be persuaded to have it at all. It is a warehouse for the demented, attending to their basic needs and storing them until they die. She cannot wait to leave.

Flo has another unhappy experience at The Gables in Thorpe, but for an altogether different reason. The Gables is a smart, mock-Tudor building standing in well-tended grounds not far from the river. The lawns are newly mown; the paths are bordered by manicured lavender hedges. A couple sits on a garden bench enjoying the spring flowers. Inside it is more like a country house than a care home. The residents are mainly retired professionals and Flo feels Arthur would be with like-minded people here. He might even enjoy it. 'Yes, we do take dementia guests, as long as they're not aggressive and not wanderers. In the daytime there are no locks on the outside doors so it would be possible for them to slip away unnoticed.' She laughs. 'And that's fine, as long as they can find their own way back. We don't want to be sending out search parties! And if their condition worsens, then sadly The Gables isn't going to be the right place for them.'

Flo's heart sinks. Arthur is a wanderer and he can be aggressive. Even if they agreed to take him at The Gables, she can't see him lasting the course. 'It's so lovely,' she says, 'but I'm afraid Dad is a wanderer and he's getting more and more confused.'

'We'd be happy to meet your dad and tell you if The Gables would be right for him.'

'That's very good of you,' says Flo, but I think it might be too unkind. A year ago The Gables would have been ideal, but Dad's gone downhill so much, and Mum's death has set him back further, even though he hardly seems to acknowledge it. I just don't know what we should do.'

When Flo reports on The Gables to Maria, she is crying down the phone.

*

A week passes. It is Flo's turn again to stay at Rose Bank and Maria makes her escape and begins her own search. The first home she visits, recommended by one of her neighbours, is in the depths of the countryside, almost at the end of a farm track. It is a ramshackle building, some of the paintwork (inevitably magnolia) is flaking and not all the rooms are en suite. However, first appearances are deceptive. It is evident that everyone on the staff – not in uniform, and with an exotic assortment of piercings and tattoos – is devoted to the place and to the residents. If it is possible to sense love, you can sense it here. 'No, we don't have any of that dementia apartheid,' says Maria's guide. 'We think it's rather cruel. Our dementia residents mix in with everyone else and we rarely have any trouble.' A broad grin crosses her face. 'At their age they're all a bit mad, aren't they, and why not? And they do try to look after each other. Shall we go and see some bedrooms?'

The bedrooms are reached through an extraordinary passageway. On each side, from floor to ceiling, the walls are ablaze with paper flowers in every shape, size and colour. 'Wow!' exclaims Maria. 'That's a surprise!'

'Extraordinary, isn't it? But the residents love it. They make the flowers themselves in one of their activities, so there are more and more. Some of them have taken to picking the flowers, and we put them back when they've gone to bed. You have to be a bit crazy to work here.'

The rooms themselves are no more than adequate, but most are brightened by pictures and furniture brought from home, and there are real fresh flowers in all of them. It is another thoughtful touch. In the dining room, it is tea-time, and a mix of residents and visitors is chattering away happily. It's like a big family, thinks Maria. She notices how the conversations are going round and round, and round again, but it doesn't seem to matter. However, she isn't sure. That evening, on the phone, she reports her visit to Flo. They are both in fits of laughter. 'It was all so uplifting in a strange sort of way,' says Maria, 'but I don't think it's Dad at all. Mind you, if Mum had lived another twenty years, it would have suited her perfectly.'

On Wednesday, Maria strikes gold at last, or believes she has. Primrose Court is a more modern care home, only four miles from where she lives. On the surface it is much like the one Flo saw in Sheringham, but Maria is impressed. 'It has a café where the residents can entertain their guests, and a bar, and a little cinema where they show films three times each week. But the best thing is an oak-panelled library. Not very big and hardly any books, but Dad could go there and try to write if he wanted. ... They do have a separate unit for their dementia residents, but they assess everyone individually, and when I told them about Dad they thought he'd probably be best placed in the main part of the home. ... I know it's a long way from you, Flo, but I do think it's worth your coming to have a look.'

Flo goes to weigh up Primrose Court and she agrees with Maria. As long as Arthur is not in the dementia unit and there is a vacancy, it might be the ideal place, and she'll just have to be the one putting up with the long drive when she wants to visit him. He will need a lot of persuading, but there is just a chance the home might sell itself.

So Flo collects Arthur and takes him to stay with Maria, as he and Mary had often done; then they will take him for a tour of Primrose Court (although they have not yet owned up to that part of the plan). He is understandably tired by the journey and even after a good night's sleep he is in awkward mood. Maria tells him they're going to see somewhere he might like to live. She is wearing a delicately pink jumper with the words 'TOUT VA BIEN' inscribed optimistically in large navy-blue letters. 'Not today, Maria. I know you … mean well, but I'm … quite all right at … Rose Bank ….' Eventually Arthur is cajoled, if it is what she and Flo want, but he can see no point. He is not for moving.

At Primrose Court they are greeted by Jeni (from 'Admissions and Marketing' according to her corporate-looking lapel badge), but Arthur is offhand and makes it plain he does not want to be there. They sit in the café, but even freshly brewed coffee and a sumptuous walnut cake do nothing to improve his humour. Jeni does not help and begins to fire questions at him from her clipboard list. Bad move, think Flo and Maria: why not show him round and get him onside first? Arthur makes no attempt to answer the questions properly; or more likely he senses danger and his lack of engagement is deliberate. Either way, he finds her East European accent hard to understand. Jeni is not impressed and makes scant effort to conceal it. 'I'll speak to Matron and we'll be in touch.'

'We'd really like Dad to have a look round,' says Flo. 'He's come all the way from Norfolk to see Primrose Court.'

'Of course,' says Jeni reluctantly (If you insist, she means). In the lounge, five well-groomed ladies are waiting patiently for the weekly quiz. 'We always wait, but it never happens,' says one, but it doesn't seem to worry them. They are taken to a bedroom: it is clean and characterless.

'Shall I take you to the dementia floor?' asks Jeni.

'No, thank you,' says Maria, 'but I know Dad would like to see the cinema and the library.'

Jeni does not look keen, but she hurries them to both. Arthur remains silent and traipses wearily in her wake. 'Is there anything else you'd like to see, Arthur?' Arthur shrugs his shoulders. He is determined to be uncooperative. She takes them back to the very smart foyer – all chrome and fake wood and expensive tiling. 'Well, it's been nice meeting you,' says Jeni without conviction. 'As I said, we'll be in touch.'

Don't bother, think Flo and Maria. It does not matter. Primrose Court is never in touch.

'Would you like to go out for lunch, Dad?' asks Maria when they are back in the car.

'That's a very ... good idea,' says Arthur, perking up immediately. 'I'm quite ... hungry. Why don't I ... treat you? I didn't think ... much of that ... what's her name? All show and no ... manners. But we put her ... back in her box, didn't we?' He chortles merrily. He is almost his old self again.

*

'Well, back to square one, Flo,' says Maria when she has said goodnight to Arthur. 'But good for Dad. He sussed out Primrose Court better than we did.'

'I suppose we wanted it too much,' says Flo. 'But where on earth do we do go from here?'

'We sleep on it, but we have to find somewhere. And it's not going to be one of these glitzy modern places. They may tick all the CQC boxes, but they miss out on the love. That crazy flower-power place knocks spots off Primrose Court.'

*

Sleeping provides no answer to the problem, but not long afterwards, when Flo is driving along the coast road to meet a friend for coffee, she passes Marsh View Care Home. She has passed it before, but from the outside it looks scruffy and she has mentally discounted it. Now, in desperation, it must be worth a look. She will call on her way back.

Marsh View is a bit scruffy on the inside too – an Edwardian house converted piecemeal as demand has increased, but it feels busy and it does not smell. Or rather it does smell, of beeswax polish and baking, just like Rose Bank after Grandma arrived. The staff are welcoming and the residents in the conservatory are a friendly lot, although much older than Arthur. He won't like all these decrepit people and they won't like the endless rambling loops of his conversation. Leading off the conservatory is a beautifully laid out walled garden, an orderly oasis of calm, so different from the unruly grounds you can see from the road. The bedrooms are individual and tasteful, the furnishings a mix of nursing-home staple and residents' own. No, the residents with dementia are not separated: 'As long as they don't upset the others, we find it's much better that way.'

'And do you have a vacancy?' asks Flo. She knows vacancies in good care homes are a matter of luck: literally waiting to fill a dead person's shoes.

'As it happens, one has just come up, a rather special ground floor room at the front. Would you like to have a look while you're here?'

Flo is immediately taken with the room, with its striped red curtains and Berber carpet. It is bathed in sunlight and she can see how some of Arthur's furniture might fit in with the oak-effect wardrobe and chest of drawers, and how some of his pictures and photographs could hang on the walls. She notices the new mattress on the bed, and on it, waiting to be made up, are blankets and an eiderdown. There was once a view of the marshes, although it is has been all but hidden by houses recently built. Outside, a blue tit is pecking at a feeder. 'What do you think?' asks Matron. 'I don't like to be pushy, but I'm afraid it won't be vacant for long.'

Flo hesitates. She doesn't want to make the decision. She wants to discuss it with Maria. She wants Arthur not to have to go into any home, ever. 'I'm just not sure,' she says, and she pours out all Arthur's troubles and all the agonies she and Maria are going through. She tells Matron of their depressing experience at Primrose Court. 'We can't do that to Dad again. It wouldn't be fair.'

Matron recognises the tiredness and despair etched into Flo's face. She has seen it so many times before. But that is why Marsh View and all the other care homes exist. 'I tell you what,' she says, 'why don't you bring your dad here for a holiday, for some respite care, and you can see how it goes? I can book you the room for a month to start with, if that helps.' It is how things usually begin. It is most likely a point of no return.

Perhaps Marsh View is the right place. It won't be easy. Arthur won't want a holiday. He'll fight against it. He can't cope with change. It's a horrid thing to do to him. 'I feel really, really guilty,' says Flo, 'but it may be the only answer. Can I speak to my sister and I'll phone you later on?' It is as if a heavy burden is lifting from her at last; at the same time another heavier one, of shame, is replacing it.

That afternoon, Flo speaks to Maria. They agree it is a plan. If it doesn't work out, they'll have to rethink, yet it will have to work out and this is how it's going to be. They have their own families and their own lives to consider. How selfish are they being? 'I'll come over at the weekend and we'll do it,' says Maria.

*

At Rose Bank, secretly, as if she is a criminal, Flo packs a battered leather suitcase for Arthur – all the things he will need for a week at Marsh View: before long they will take in other things, but too much at once would make him even more suspicious. She tells him she and

I Am Arthur Bright

Maria are taking their families away for a break and so she is booking a holiday for him too. A hotel on the north coast where they will look after him properly. 'You need a break as well, Dad,' she says.

'Well, I'll come ... with you.'

'I'm afraid you can't, Dad, the flight would be far too long for you.' There is no flight. It frightens Flo how the lies trip off her tongue.

'Then, I'll stay ... at home. I'll manage ok ... by myself. You go and enjoy yourselves ... without me. Send me a postcard.' He stomps off into the garden. Flo feels terrible.

At breakfast the next morning, Arthur has forgotten all about the holiday, so they have to repeat the whole unedifying performance. I won't bother to tell him again, thinks Flo. It's not worth it. At lunch, Arthur says he's thinking of going on holiday. Would all the family like to come too? He'd like the company. In the evening, Maria arrives. 'Don't mention the holiday,' whispers Flo. 'It only makes things worse.'

It is Saturday – departure day. Without Arthur knowing it, Flo puts his case into the boot of the car. 'Come on, Dad. We're going out.'

Arthur is all smiles. 'That'll be ... nice.' He sits in the back with Maria, while Flo drives.

After a couple of miles, 'It's like going on ... holiday,' says Arthur.

'You are going on holiday, Dad,' says Flo from the front. 'Don't you remember, you're going to stay on the north coast for a week or two? It'll be lovely.'

For a few seconds there is silence. Then, 'I told you, I don't want ... to go,' says Arthur.

'It'll be great, Dad,' says Maria. 'You've always liked the marshes.'

'I don't want ... to go,' he shouts, and he grabs the door handle, struggling to get out. Luckily, the door is locked. 'You're ... kidnapping me.' His features change. They become hard, even vicious. He is fighting for everything he is having to leave behind.

Flo keeps driving. She does not want to go on, but turning back would be turning into an abyss. 'Look at the marshes, Dad,' says Maria. Arthur rattles the door handle. 'You ungrateful children!' They pull up outside Marsh View. 'Here we are, Dad,' says Maria. 'I'm sure you'll like it. Let's get you settled in, shall we?' She gets out, retrieves Arthur's suitcase, opens the door on Arthur's side. 'Come on, Dad, let me give you a hand.'

'I am not getting out,' Arthur says to himself. 'I am not getting out,' he says aloud, almost with a snarl.

Flo and Maria plead, cajole, become impatient. They are angry and tearful. 'Don't do this to us, Dad. It's only for a short time and you'll enjoy it.' More lies tumble out. Arthur looks away and says nothing. Somewhere, struggling to the surface of his mind, is the time he was extracted from Grandpa's car at Sparrowhawk Hall, with no idea what was happening to him. He is not falling for that trick again.

Flo goes to the home to ask for help. She is embarrassed and upset. A young lady, smart in a sky-blue uniform, answers the door. 'Good morning. Can I help?' she asks smilingly.

'We've brought our dad, Arthur Bright, to stay at Cathedral View but we can't get him out of the car. It's so silly, but we don't know what to do.'

'Oh good, we're expecting Arthur,' says the young lady, not at all perturbed. 'Let me come and meet him. Some of our residents find it a bit difficult at first, but they do settle in quite quickly.' She walks with them back to the car. 'Hello, Arthur,' she says. 'Have you come to have a holiday with us? I'm Alice.'

Arthur looks up at her. A friendly face. Not Mrs Cholmondeley-Robinson. 'Alice ... in wonderland?'

'That's right, Arthur, Alice in wonderland. We've really been looking forward to meeting you. Are you going to come in? You're just in time for coffee and some scrummy cake.'

'I think perhaps ... I will. If it's not too ... much trouble.'

Alice takes his arm and helps him up. She picks up his suitcase. 'Thank you for bringing him,' says Alice and, almost in a whisper, 'If you'd like to pop back in half an hour or so, Matron will do all the paperwork with you. ... Come along, Arthur.'

Arthur walks off meekly with her. He does not look back. 'Did you say your name ... was Alice?' he asks.

'Yes, Arthur. Alice in wonderland.'

'Easy as that!' says Maria, as they watch Arthur trotting off arm-in-arm with Alice. 'Dad's always fallen for a pretty girl!'

A little later, Matron goes through the details of Arthur's stay, gives them a Marsh View handbook and an extraordinarily large invoice for the coming month. She is business-like, but sympathetic and reassuring. The twins gain the impression that she runs a tight ship: they will do as they are told. 'It's best if you don't visit for the first week. Just let your dad get used to us. I'm sure it will work out, and then you can bring in some of his favourite bits and pieces to make the room more homely. ... If possible, we like to have some photographs and anything else from the past we can talk to him about. ... Are there any particular likes or dislikes we need to know?'

'He's not fussy about food,' says Flo. 'But he does like a glass of sherry before his supper if it's allowed.'

'I'm sure we can manage that. He's not the only one! I'll phone you tomorrow, if that's all right, to let you know how he's getting on.'

Flo and Maria have an empty feeling as they leave and the door clicks shut. They are desperately worried how Arthur will cope. 'Come on, let's get back,' says Flo wearily. 'I could do with a very stiff drink.'

*

Alice takes Arthur to his room. It is light and airy, but a little old-fashioned: it could be a room in any pleasant provincial hotel. 'I'm sure you'll have a lovely holiday here, Arthur. Why don't you sit down and I'll fetch us a coffee and some cake. Then I can help you unpack if you like.' While Alice hurries out, leaving the door open, Arthur goes across to the window, watches the birds, can just make out the distant marshes. They have always been one of his special places. He sits down on the bed and puts his pounding head in his hands. He feels terribly alone. He did not want to come here and does not understand why. Anyway, the girls will be back to collect him. Alice returns: there is coffee for them both, a jug of milk, a bowl of sugar lumps and some home-made cake. She sits down next to him. 'How do you take your coffee, Arthur?'

'With some ... milk, please. Where am I?'

Alice doesn't quite answer. 'You've come for a holiday with us, so we can look after you while your daughters are away.'

'Like ... putting a dog ... in kennels?'

'No, it's not like that, Arthur. Most people like it so much they decide to live here all the time.'

'Do you live here?'

'I spend some nights here, but I've also got my own flat just down the road.'

'What sort of ... place is this? Does my ... mother ... know I'm here?'

'I'm sure she does, Arthur. Would you like some of this delicious cake?'

'Just a small slice,' says Arthur. In time he will become used to this cake, a rather heavy Victoria sandwich with thin, seedless jam.

Alice puts a slice on a plate for him and lays a serviette on his lap. She makes conversation. It was nice to meet his daughters. What are their names? Do they live nearby? What did he do for a job? Has he been to this part of Norfolk before? She gives Arthur time to answer, but today he is particularly confused. It is often like this when a new resident arrives, but give it time. ... She takes his mug and plate and puts them back on the tray. 'Shall I help you unpack your case?'

'I don't ... think so,' says Arthur slowly. 'I won't be staying.'

'Only for a few nights, but let's hang up your jacket and trousers and put your shirts into the drawer. We don't want them to get creased, do we?'

Arthur watches on helplessly as what are left of his belongings are unpacked and put away. He has no strength left to complain. Alice slides his suitcase under the bed. 'That's better, Arthur. All done. Would you like to come along to the conservatory to meet some of our other guests? Or would you rather stay and relax for a bit? There are some nice magazines you could look at. It'll be lunchtime soon — if you're not too full of cake.'

'I'd rather stay here ... if you don't mind,' says Arthur. 'What did you say your ... name was?'

'Alice.'

'Alice ... in wonderland?'

'Yes, Arthur. Alice in wonderland.'

Arthur tries to stand up. 'I must go to see ... my mother,' he says.

*

'Time for lunch, Arthur,' says Alice cheerfully. Arthur is still sitting on the bed. 'Come on, let me help you up and I'll show you the way. The others are looking forward to meeting you.' Arthur looks up at her, resigned, lost. He stands up and walks with her along the passageway. The carpet has a broad yellow line running down the centre. 'You just follow the yellow line,' says Alice. 'Follow the yellow brick road! It takes you to the dining room, and the conservatory, and the office. So you'll always be able to find people.' Arthur can hear the hubbub of the dining room. He does not want to go in, but Alice is persuasive. Most of the thirty residents are here, sitting at six yellow tables. 'Here's a place for you, Arthur,' she says, taking him to a vacant chair. 'This is George on your right. ... George, this is Arthur who's come to join us.'

"Pleased to meet you.' George offers his hand. Arthur ignores it and says nothing. 'Suit yourself,' says George.

'And this is Linda on your left.'

Linda is small and red-faced, with wispy hair, smudged lipstick and whiskers on her chin. 'Hello, dear,' says Linda. 'Welcome to the Marsh View madhouse!' and she cackles like a witch.

'Don't worry about her,' says the lady sitting next to her. 'She's the only mad one here. Aren't you, Linda?'

One of the ladies sitting opposite Arthur has her head bowed, almost resting it on the table; the other has picked up her knife and fork and is eating something invisible.

'Cottage pie today,' says George. 'It's Saturday.'

Cottage pie and peas arrive at the table. Linda cackles.

Arthur looks round the room. It is like school lunch, but twice as noisy. He won't stand for it. He brings his fist down hard on the table. 'Silence!' he tries to shout. 'Let's have some ... silence in here!' There is a surprised and momentary lull, and then the noise returns. Arthur is struggling to stand. Intentionally or by accident, he sweeps his arm across the table and tumblers, cutlery, and half-eaten food crash onto the floor. Linda claps her hands in glee; no-one else takes much notice. George plods on doggedly with his cottage pie, which has managed to escape Arthur's attention.

Alice appears at Arthur's side. 'Oh dear, Arthur,' she says. 'What a shame. Let's go and tidy you up.' Arthur does not need tidying up, but he does need rescuing. She takes him back to his room. 'I wonder what happened, Arthur. Shall I fetch your lunch in here for you?'

Arthur shakes his head, turns his back, curls up on the bed and pulls the eiderdown over him. When Alice looks in at teatime, before she goes home, Arthur is still asleep. At suppertime, when Matron checks on him, he is beginning to stir. 'How are you feeling, Arthur?' she asks brightly.

'I think I must have ... been asleep. What sort of ... time is it?'

'Yes, you've been asleep for some time. 'It's nearly seven o'clock. I'm sure you must be hungry. Would you like me to bring you some supper?'

'That would be nice. ... But aren't I ... going home today?'

'No, Arthur, you're staying with us for a few days' holiday while Flo and Maria are away.'

Arthur looks confused. 'Are you sure?'

'I'm quite sure, Arthur, but don't worry, we'll look after you. You'll have a super time here. I'll bring you some supper in a minute. And how about a small glass of sherry first?'

'You're ... very kind,' says Arthur.

'I'll put the radio on, shall I? Would you like the news or some music?'

'Music, perhaps. ... It's more cheerful ... than the news.'

On the radio they are playing a Beatles' song:

> *Hey Jude, don't make it bad.*
> *Take a sad song and make it better.*

As it happens, it is one of his favourites. Aboard *Still Waters*, all those years ago, Mary would strum her guitar and she and Arthur would sing along to it. Arthur's face lightens. Alzheimer's has so far failed to steal all the lyrics from him and he begins to join in uncertainly, humming when the words desert him. He is happily tapping his feet when Matron returns with his sherry. 'I do need to see ... my mother,' he says.

*

On Sunday evening, the phone rings and after a few seconds Flo answers it with some trepidation. 'Hello, Flo Johnston speaking.'

'Hello, Flo. It's Matron from Marsh View. I promised I'd ring you.'

'Thank you so much,' says Flo. 'I haven't been able to stop wondering about Dad. How's he getting on?'

'He's fine. He's just had his supper and I've popped in to see him. He's listening to the radio and looking through a magazine.'

'Is he settling in all right, then?'

'It's still early days, but we hope he'll be very happy at Marsh View,' says Matron. (Flo notices the slight hesitation and the 'hope': why hasn't she answered the question?). 'He did find the dining room rather daunting at lunch yesterday and he had a sleep in the afternoon; but in the evening he was very chatty, and he had his glass of sherry and a good supper.'

'And what about today?'

'Well, he's chosen to have his meals in his room, but we wrapped him up well (like a parcel, thinks Flo) and took him out into the garden to enjoy the sunshine.'

'So no problems?'

'Not really. We just need to find some kindred spirits your dad's happy to talk to. Of course, we let our residents choose for themselves, but we don't want him to spend too much time by himself in his room.'

'There's nothing for us to worry about, then?'

'No, Flo, nothing that isn't normal. Dad's bound to find the change a challenge, but I'm sure he'll get used to everything.' Matron does not tell Flo that when Alice took in his coffee this morning, Arthur had retrieved his suitcase from under the bed and was all packed up and ready to be collected. 'I'll phone again on Tuesday and, if he's feeling more at home, it should be all right if you want to visit him next weekend.'

Flo is not entirely reassured, but it could have been worse. 'I had the impression Dad's being a bit awkward,' she tells Maria when she speaks to her later. 'Heaven knows what he's been getting up to. But they haven't expelled him, so we must just keep our fingers crossed.'

When Matron phones again, she does not mention how Arthur has made another bid to escape: he managed to reach the front hall

I Am Arthur Bright

with his suitcase and was struggling with the door to get out. 'We're pleased with the way your dad's going,' she says. 'Yes, do come and see him at the weekend, if it's convenient, and if you can find some of his belongings to make the room more homely, I'm sure it would help.'

'Perhaps we could bring his small writing desk and chair, and some pictures and photographs?'

'That sounds just right. Too much makes it difficult to clean.'

It is a tremendous relief for Flo. If they want Dad's things, it's unlikely they're going to throw him out. Yet her overwhelming emotion is one of profound sadness. She can hear the prison door clanging shut behind him.

*

Thus, on the following Sunday, Flo and her husband, David, arrive at Marsh View. They report to the office, sign the obligatory visitors' book, and Joan takes them along the 'yellow-brick-road' to Arthur's room. His name, 'Arthur Bright', has been put neatly on the door. 'Looks as if he's here to stay,' says David. Inside, Arthur is sitting in his chair, his back towards them, thumbing idly through a copy of *Norfolk Life* and listening to the radio.

'Hello, Dad. How are you?'

Arthur glances over his shoulder. 'Flo? They told me … you might be … coming. Are you going to … take me home?'

'Not today, Dad. But we've brought you one or two of your belongings.'

'I can … pack, but I'm not sure … where they've put my … case.'

'No, Dad, we've been looking forward to seeing where you're living. It's a lovely place you've found.'

Arthur is puzzled. He peers around him. 'I suppose it is … rather nice. A bit dull, though, isn't it? It could do with … livening up a bit. I'm not quite sure how … I got here.'

'We've brought some of your pictures for you, Dad. David will put them up if you like. Why don't you show me round while he does it?'

'There's not that much to … show,' he says, but he stands up slowly. It is Flo who leads the way. They go to the dining room, which is being laid up for lunch. 'I don't … come here. Too noisy.'

'It's roast chicken today, Arthur,' says one of the ladies.

'Good. I like chicken. … And roast potatoes?'

'Of course. And all the trimmings. Why don't you have it in here?'

'Maybe … another time.'

They walk through to the conservatory where there is a bubbling of animated chatter and someone is tangled up in a Sunday broadsheet. 'This is nice, Dad. Do you come in here, then?'

Arthur shakes his head. 'Too many … old people,' he says loudly. Flo cringes, but either they have not heard him or they are not bothered. They go out into the walled garden. 'I like it here,' says Arthur. … 'Peaceful.'

Arthur and Flo sit on a teak garden bench. It has that rich, oily scent. Not far away, three other residents are enjoying the sunshine. Flo notices there is a door in the wall, which leads to the outside world, but thank goodness it is locked. No chance of getting out. The garden is alive with late spring flowers, daffodils and tulips beginning to go over. They remind Flo of the garden at Rose Bank and her eyes moisten. They talk of this and that, this and that, this and that, round and round and round. The same questions and the same answers. Arthur does not know where he is and Flo is vague in her replies. After a while, David emerges from the conservatory. 'Here you are! I thought I'd lost you. What a magnificent garden, Arthur. It must be a lot of work for you.' A robin flies onto the rose arbour, plumps up his chest and chirrups joyfully.

'Are you coming in for lunch, Arthur?' calls Joan 'You want it in your room, I suppose?'

Arthur nods. 'Thank you.'

David has transformed the room. Arthur's writing desk has fitted in near the window, so the light falls on its green leather top and picks out the gold inlay. Long ago, Mary had bought the desk for him at an auction. The watercolour of Norwich market, the leaving gift from Spinney Hill, hangs above it and there is another watercolour of 'Widgeon over the Marshes'. Beside his bed there is a photograph of Mary standing proudly outside her antique shop. More will follow, but they do not want to overwhelm him. Arthur seems uncertain, but he is pleased when Joan brings his lunch and he tucks into it eagerly. There is jam roly-poly and custard to follow. Flo has worried that Arthur will be upset when they leave and fail to take him with them, but it has been a busy morning and after lunch, as he begins to doze, they are able to slip away. Joan unlocks the door to let them out. 'He's beginning to settle in,' she says. 'We just wish he'd mix in with the others, but it's hard when he's so much younger than most of them.'

'Well, thank you for looking after him,' says Flo. 'It's a weight off our shoulders.'

'He doesn't seem too bad,' says David as they head for home. 'I think I'd be happy enough there if they fed me like that. I haven't had jam roly-poly since I was at school.'

*

Next Saturday it is Maria who pays Arthur a visit. She brings him flowers and a box of 'Black Magic' chocolates. 'My favourites, Flo,' he says, taking the box from her.

'I'm Maria, not Flo,' she says, chuckling.

'Are you ... Fore or ... Aft?'

'Aft, Dad. Daft Aft! Ready to set sail, captain!' Maria is astounded. How does he remember Fore and Aft (in reality, the names they had chosen as children were the wrong way round: Flo was always the daft one, and Maria was more serious, like her father)? 'But what a lovely place you've got, Dad. Clever you! Your pictures are perfect, and look at your desk! You should start writing again. And what a glorious wisteria outside! I'll go and ask for a vase for the flowers.' Just as Arthur had done with Flo, they make a tour of Marsh View. Arthur is still not sure where he is, but he is apparently untroubled. When Maria goes to the office to borrow a vase for the flowers, Matron is positive. 'He has good days and bad days,' she says. 'On the bad days he puts himself to bed and wakes up right as rain.'

'Well, he seems fine now,' says Maria. 'I just hope I'm not upsetting him.'

'He'll love seeing you, but if he's not asleep when you leave, it's best to make an excuse and say you'll be back. It sounds dreadfully underhand, I know, but after a few minutes he won't be waiting for you and I'm afraid he won't even remember you've been.'

Maria spends the night at Flo's. On Sunday, before she returns home, they drive in separate cars to Rose Bank. They need to make sure it is secure and there is much tidying of the garden to be done. Flo is wearing an old tee shirt and jeans, ready for a work party. Maria is wearing a summery dress, as if for a garden party. It has always been like this, but they get on well. The house is full of ghosts from the past – the carefree childhood days and the agonies and ecstasies of adolescence. They miss their Mum dreadfully – it shouldn't have happened like that – and now, bit by bit, Dad is drifting away from them into his own mixed-up world where there is neither past nor future. After lunch they spend their time leafing through papers and photographs, trying to pick out the ones that will help Arthur cling to his old life for a little longer. 'Wouldn't it be nice if we made them into a book?' says Maria. 'Dad's story. So he has something to look through and we can talk about it when we visit him.' Flo agrees, but because Maria lives so far away and the burden of visiting Arthur will fall more heavily on Flo, it is Maria who will work on a first draft. As the evening shadows fall, she gathers up the remnants of Arthur's life and puts them into a large white envelope. 'Dad's Story', she writes on it, and for the journey home she puts it on the passenger seat beside her.

Flo takes Arthur's address book: she will inform his closest friends he has moved: most of them will not be surprised. Rose Bank will have to be cleared and sold, but they will not tell Dad and they cannot bring themselves to do it yet. Arthur will not be coming back, but it has all been too sudden and too upsetting. They need time to grieve for their Mum, and in a way for their Dad; they need time to give back to their husbands and children, and time to come to terms with what they have done; and then one day (although they cannot imagine it yet) they hope they will be able to move on.

VIII

In the Walled Garden

Eventually Arthur does settle at Marsh View, but not before Flo and Maria have spent anguished weeks believing they have made a mistake. He has been stubborn in his refusal to eat in the dining room or to mix with the other residents at all; when they visit, he begs them to take him home, although already he has no idea where home might be; he continues to obsess about his mother. Matron tries to be reassuring: some people take longer than others to adapt to this new way of life and everyone has to be given choice: it is detrimental and inconvenient, but he cannot be dragged out for meals against his will. He is well cared for and the doctor has no concerns about his physical health. Of course, the room may be given up at any time with very little notice, but Flo and Maria can think of no alternative. They have seen for themselves that Marsh View is more suitable for Arthur than anywhere else they have found, and it gives him the attention and stability they know they cannot give him themselves. The other residents appear to enjoy Marsh View (although there may be some who, like Arthur, rarely emerge) and the visitors they meet cannot speak more highly of the way their relatives are looked after. 'We went through the same at the beginning, but he'll be all right soon, you'll see.' No, they will wait a little longer and hope things improve. Meanwhile they dread the days when they come to see Arthur. Maria, especially, suffers hours of driving, wondering what she will find; if it turns out to be one of his bad days, he will retreat under his eiderdown and refuse to speak, and it is a wasted journey. Would it matter if she did not come? After all, Dad never remembers when she has been. It is an unworthy question, quickly dismissed. Neither she, nor Flo, will ever abandon him, although they feel they already have.

It is predictably Alice who plays the major part in drawing Arthur out of the doldrums. She sees how he relaxes when he is listening to music and she is always trying to find what he enjoys on the radio. She suggests to Flo that she brings a CD player and some of Arthur's discs – or better still makes some compilations of what he likes best. 'No problem,' says Flo, who feels it is something positive she can do. To an extent the music is a success: it relieves Arthur's boredom and raises his battered spirits; but it does not move him from his room.

'Would you like to come to a concert with me, Arthur?' asks Alice one day. 'There's music in the lounge this afternoon and I'm sure you'd enjoy it.'

'I don't ... think so. I'm quite ... all right here.'

'Oh, do come, Arthur. I don't want to go on my own. I'll sit with you and you can bring me back here for tea afterwards. What do you say? Please, Arthur.'

Arthur looks up at her face, which is willing him to agree. 'If you have no one else to go with ... I suppose ...' It is not in his nature to disappoint her.

'Thank you, Arthur. That's so kind of you. I'll come and collect you after lunch and we can go along together.'

When Alice leads Arthur into the lounge, he hesitates, pulls back. The concert is a popular activity at Marsh View and he does not like so many people. 'Don't worry, Arthur, we'll slip in here at the back.' She has it all worked out.

At the keyboard is oleaginous Sidney Smith. In the summer season he performs, smooth and suited, at the tourist hotels in Sheringham and Cromer – a competent but failed musician, scraping a living. He begins to play. It sounds like a fairground organ. Sidney sings the verses in a passable tenor voice and brings in everyone for the chorus. The residents are used to this. It is how the singing starts every week and it takes them back to their own seaside holidays:

> *Oh! I do like to be beside the seaside!*
> *I do like to be beside the sea!*
> *Oh I do like to stroll along the Prom, Prom, Prom!*
> *Where the brass bands play, 'Tiddely-om-pom-pom!'*
> *So just let me be beside the seaside!*
> *I'll be beside myself with glee and there's lots of girls beside,*
> *I should like to be beside, beside the seaside, beside the sea!*

And it takes Arthur back to those seaside days in Skeggy with Grandpa and Grandma, and the band played it on the promenade, and they sang it on the train going home. He knows the words and begins to join in, and Alice takes his hand and she sings, too. But how does he still know and how can he join in when speaking has become such a struggle? It is another mystery of the disease.

There are more old favourites, which Sidney plays in different styles, and there are song sheets in large print for those who want them: 'Tiptoe through the tulips', 'Carolina moon', 'I did it my way', 'Downtown', 'Lily the Pink', and so many others, and the residents call out their own requests. 'What's that, love? I can't quite hear you.' Finally, before they go off for their tea, they sing 'We'll meet again', as they always do. It could be 1945 and VE Day, when some of them were waving their flags in Trafalgar Square. If only there were flags to wave now. If only they had something to celebrate:

> *We'll meet again*
> *Don't know where*
> *Don't know when*
> *But I know we'll meet again some sunny day.*

'Let's go and get you some tea, Arthur,' says Alice and she takes him back to his room. 'That was great, wasn't it? Did you enjoy it? I didn't know you had such a good voice.'

'Can I take you … the concert … next time?' asks Arthur.

'You bet! I'd be honoured, Arthur. It's a date!'

Next time comes and Arthur does take Alice again, or she takes him. But she also takes Yvonne, a new resident at Marsh View, recently widowed, much the same age as Arthur and, like him, a sufferer from Alzheimer's who can no longer live by herself. Naturally Alice has an ulterior motive: she hopes they will strike up a friendship and Arthur will be lured from his room more often. Sidney plays most of the old favourites again and some new ones. 'Jerusalem' is sung with particular gusto by the ladies in their thin soprano voices: it had been a regular at their Women's Institute meetings and evokes cakes and home-made jam more than anything religious. It had been a regular in the Burgoyne chapel as well, along with 'Onward Christian soldiers' and 'I vow to thee, my country', and for Arthur it evokes instead the whole brutal ethos of the place: history has taught him that religion and brutality have always been strange bedfellows. But he enjoys himself and so does Yvonne, and between the songs they begin to converse – only by way of getting to know a little about each other, and the conversation is, of course, circular, and neither will remember anything of it.

Before long, when the weather improves, Alice persuades Arthur to go for a walk with her in the walled garden. He likes the garden but hasn't the confidence to go there by himself. It is June and the roses are already in bloom, honeysuckle, jasmine, and glorious clematis cling to the walls, and disordered cottage flowers squeeze into the borders. There are scarlet geraniums in old oak barrels and busy lizzies tumbling from the hanging baskets. Some of the residents help in the garden, although they are limited in what they can do, but now some are sitting on the silvery benches, reading or dozing, or letting the summer heat nourish their sun-starved skin and hoping it will last. Arthur always liked the garden at Rose Bank, and does the walled garden stir in him any thoughts of the undistant past? Alice helps him walk along the limestone path; they rest in the small gazebo and listen to the birdsong. Not many days are so perfect.

'I do think Yvonne would like it in the garden,' says Alice. 'Do you remember Yvonne? She sat with us at the concert last week'

Arthur wrinkles his brow. 'Did she? I don't ... recall.'

'I ought to go and find her? You don't mind, do you, Arthur? You stay here, and I'll be back in a jiffy.'

Arthur does mind – he would rather have Alice to himself – but he is too polite to object; and after a while Alice comes back with Yvonne, and with a tray of coffee and shortbread. She pours the coffee and leaves. Arthur and Yvonne talk, admire the flowers, sleep, talk, watch the slow comings and goings of their fellows, admire the flowers. Alice returns. 'I tell you what. Would you both like your lunch out here? We could put a table outside the conservatory.'

'That would be ... very nice, don't you think, Arthur?' says Yvonne. Arthur is not sure but remains silent. More than once, Matron has warned Alice not to grow too close to the residents and she knows that her cunning plans are resented by many of her colleagues. But she sees how Alice has a special empathy and does not want to curb her enthusiasm, and she wishes some of the others would be as thoughtful and work as hard. They are lucky to have her at Marsh View.

Alice carries a small table outside and lays it up for three. She is going to persuade George to join them. She sits them down. 'That's very ... kind, dear,' says Yvonne.

Alice puts her hand on Arthur's shoulder. 'All right, Arthur?'

Joan brings their lunch – a chicken casserole, with peas, carrots and a rich gravy – and plonks it down in front of them. 'Well, you're the chosen ones, aren't you?'

'I like it in ... the garden,' says Arthur. Yvonne gives Joan an old-fashioned look. George tucks into his casserole.

The warm weather continues and in days to come there are two tables outside. Matron comes out and looks on approvingly. Alice has succeeded in luring Arthur out of his room and he seems altogether more settled. When it rains, the two tables are set up just inside the conservatory, a fraction away from the clatter of the dining room. Why didn't we think of this before? It's so much better for our younger guests.

'Where would you like your lunch today, Arthur?' asks bustling Joan. 'In your room?'

'In the … conservatory … if it's not too much trouble.'

'No problem. You like it there, don't you?' La-di-da, she thinks. Alice means well, but she just makes work for everyone.

*

Visitors come. Flo comes two or three times a week, Maria once a month, sometimes with Jill and John. Arthur recognises the twins and is delighted to see them; he does not recognise his grandchildren, but 'Of course!' he says when they tell him. It is much easier in the garden, when they do not have to try so hard to make conversation, and they can walk with him on the gravel path and admire the flowers. 'You had roses like these at Rose Bank, didn't you, Grandad?' says Jill.

'Did I? Rose Bank … is where I used … to live, isn't it?'

'A long time ago. But it's so nice here in this beautiful garden.'

'It is … isn't it?' If Arthur cannot at first remember Rose Bank, he can remember the roses and a hazy picture begins to emerge. 'Did you … live there?'

'No, Mum and Auntie Flo lived there when they were little, didn't they?'

'If you say so … Did you live there?'

'Look at those glorious peonies, Grandad,' says Jill.

*

One wet day, Norman arrives. 'Hello, Arthur. How are you? What a great place you've got here.'

Arthur studies him. 'I'm not sure ...'

'It's Norman. From Hartbourne.'

'Norman. ... Yes. ... It's good to ... see you ... Norman.'

'How are you keeping? You look well.'

'I can't complain. ... It looks a bit ... miserable ... out there.'

'It is a bit rainy. So, what've you been doing with yourself, Arthur? I haven't seen you for a long time.'

'Not much. ... I don't get out much these days. ... I think ... I did walk down to ... the river yesterday.'

There is no river near Marsh View. Norman knows Arthur's mind is playing its tricks, but does it matter? 'It was better weather yesterday, wasn't it? Are there still lots of boats?'

'A few.'

'You used to live on a boat with Mary, didn't you? *Still Waters*, wasn't it? I came to stay with you a few times – on that sofa bed!'

'Did you? I hope it wasn't ... too bad. ... I haven't seen ... Mary ... for some time. Have you?'

A pause. 'No, Arthur, not recently. I haven't been this way.'

'Did you say ... you've seen ... Mary? ... I hope she ... comes soon. ... 'Where do ... live now?'

'I'm still at Hartbourne. You'd hardly know it, it's changed so much. There are two vast new housing estates on the Grantham Road. The houses are like little boxes, all crammed next to each other. Even so, there aren't many buses to Grantham now and the shop closed last year. That was a big loss.'

Hartbourne is on the bottom shelf of Dr Patel's bookcase and Arthur can just about picture it. 'A pity. ... It used to ... sell everything. ... Do you still ... see ... anyone else?'

'Not really anyone from the old days. I do occasionally see Sarah. She used to live next door to you.' Although Norman would not want to admit it, he has, over the years, fallen with increasing regularity into

Sarah's amorous clutches. In fact they have become quite close. (Oh, Mary, if only you had known.)

Of course, Arthur does remember Sarah and the day he went for a picnic with her. The day has lost the power to disturb him, but sixty years on he is still not going to tell. 'Rather a … floozy, wasn't she? But I did … like her.'

'Perhaps I'll bring her with me next time. She'd love to see you.'

'Why not? I'll look forward … to it.'

As Mary had predicted, Sarah had not settled in Watermouth. If you were not at the University it was just another deprived seaside town, and depressing in winter when the holidaymakers had left, leaving only their litter behind, and the arcades and souvenir shops were closed and shuttered. However, she had stayed long enough to acquire and discard a wealthy husband. He had cheated on her; she had cheated on him, too, but he had never discovered. Within three years she had returned to Grantham, richer but not wiser, married again, had two delightfully wayward daughters whom she did little to control, eventually discarded her second husband, became a trendy grandmother, and now contents herself with a whirl of cinema outings, cocktail parties and dinner dates, often with Norman as a decorative accoutrement. If she is bored, she will scroll through a dating app for the 'young at heart'. Probably she has never loved anyone apart from her daughters, but her hedonistic lifestyle has not yet caught up with her and she admits to no regrets.

Arthur is quiet, closes his eyes, sees again the picnic at Galleons Lap and the supper at Aunt Dorothy's. 'Do you know … what happened … to Sarah?' he asks.

*

Later that summer, Flo asks Matron if it would be all right to take Arthur out for a day. He has been at Marsh View for four months and, although Alice has been working wonders, he is probably not yet altogether happy. A stroll on the saltmarsh and lunch at a pub might cheer him up. Matron hesitates. 'It's so difficult to tell,' she says. 'I'm sure he'd enjoy it and it could do him good, but it might unsettle him if he's out of routine. ... It has to be up to you.'

Not very helpful, thinks Flo. But it is up to her. She talks to David and to Maria. On balance, they think it is worth the risk. The guilt of moving Arthur into Marsh View has not left Flo and she owes him. She phones Matron and tells her she is going to give it a try. 'How about on Monday?' suggests Matron. 'There'll be the usual concert on Tuesday, so he'll have that to enjoy the next day.'

Monday comes and Arthur is surprisingly reluctant. 'No, thank you Flo, it's a very ... nice thought, but I'd prefer to ... stay here, if you ... don't mind.'

'But you love the marshes, Dad, and you haven't been there for ages.'

'I'll think ... about it. ... Maybe ... next week.'

Eventually Arthur is persuaded. Alice helps him to the car. 'Are you ... coming with us, Alice?'

'I'm afraid not, Arthur. I've got my work to do here.'

'Are you ... sure?'

'Quite sure, Arthur. I'll see you later. Have a lovely day.' She asks Flo when they plan to be back. 'I'll look out for you. Be good, Arthur!'

Arthur sits in the front next to Flo. He is uneasy, suspicious. There was the time Grandpa and Grandma had taken him in the car to Sparrowhawk. And there was another time when he was put into a car and taken somewhere he didn't want to go. 'Are you sure it's all right, Flo?'

'It's fine, Dad. We're going to have a walk on the marshes and lunch at a pub. Then we're coming home for tea.' But Flo is herself confused. It's good that Dad feels safe at Marsh View and seems at last to think of it as some sort of home; but it's frightening how he's become institutionalised so quickly and is worried about going out.

Should she be doing this more often or not doing it at all?

They drive the short distance to Cley, where the view stretches across the marshes, and park in the beach car park. Flo helps Arthur out and they sit in the sunshine and look out across the Wash. The sea is calm and there are boats dotted along the coast. They talk about nothing in particular: Flo notices Dad's speech has become slower and he is even more repetitive, but he is in good spirits. They drive back to the pub in Cley and sit outside; Flo orders crab sandwiches and a small shandy for them both. Local crab: it is what Arthur and Mary always enjoyed: 'There's nothing wrong with your appetite, Dad!' They stay on for a little, but clouds are rolling in and Flo decides it is time to go back.

'Here we are, home again,' says Flo as they turn into the drive at Marsh View. The rain is beginning to fall.

Arthur becomes agitated. 'This isn't ... home. Where are ... you taking me?'

'Of course, it's home, Dad. You've lived here for some time now.'

'No I haven't. You're ... trying to ... put me away.' Has he seen the sign which says 'Marsh View Care Home'?

'Take me back ... to my ... own home,' he says.

Flo does not argue. She sees all the good the day has done beginning to ebb away and she won't be repeating this in a hurry. She has no idea how she will get Arthur out of the car without a struggle. Then Alice is walking towards them. She opens Arthur's door. 'Hello, Arthur. Welcome home. I've been waiting for you. Let me help you out. ... Did you have a nice day?'

'Very ... nice ... thank you,' says Arthur, taking her arm.

'Bye, Dad,' calls Flo. 'See you soon.' She breathes a sigh of relief. Alice is a marvel. Arthur does not even look back.

'Where did you go, Arthur?' asks Alice as she takes him in and back to his room.

Arthur thinks for a while, 'I'm not ... sure.'

'And did you have a lovely lunch?'

'I don't think we ... had ... lunch.'

'I'm sure you did, Arthur. But it's nearly teatime, so you won't go hungry.'

'Good. ... I'd like a ... cup of tea. Will ... Mary ... be here for ... tea? ... We had ... crab sandwiches.'

*

In August, Ray arrives. 'Hi, Arthur. How are you getting on? Cute little place you've got yourself.'

Arthur looks up from his chair. He has been browsing through his book: he only looks at the photographs now. 'Not bad, is it? ... I'm not sure how I found it. ... Very nice people.' He looks puzzled. 'Have we met?'

'It's Ray, Arthur.' Ray has barely changed, but he notices how much older and frailer Arthur has become. 'How are you keeping?'

'I can't ... complain.'

'And what've you been getting up to?'

'Not much. ... I don't go ... very far ... these days. I did have a ... walk by the river ... this morning.'

'I bet it's changed.'

'Has it? I haven't ... noticed.'

'And what about Flo and Maria. How are they doing?'

'All right, I believe. I haven't ... seen them ... for a while.'

Ray speaks to Flo regularly. He knows it is not true, but lets it pass. 'So what's the book you're reading, Arthur?' Arthur hands it to him. 'Wow! *I Am Arthur Bright*! Your story!' He leafs through the pages. 'I've never seen some of these pictures, Arthur. Your dear mother looks a charmer! ... And look at you in your soldier's uniform! Very smart! ... That's the University, isn't it? That's where I first met you with Mary. ... And there's *Still Waters*. They were good times, weren't they? You and Mary were so happy there. ... And that's your wedding! That's me, being your "best man". It was a great day. ... That's you and Mary going off on your honeymoon. You must miss Mary. She was a lovely girl. You were very lucky.'

'Did you get married?' asks Arthur.

'Yes, I did, not that long ago. Geoff, my husband, is a great guy. You must meet him.'

Arthur is muddled by it all. He can remember his mother. He can just remember The Burgoyne School – a dreadful place. But *Still Waters* and Mary are insubstantial shadows, appearing and disappearing. And how does Ray have a husband called Geoff? 'Have you seen ... Mary today?' he asks.

Ray ignores the question. He continues to look through the photographs, sharing them with Arthur and trying as best he can to draw him into conversation. Sometimes Arthur's face lights up briefly as a place or a person takes shape, but it is desperately sad how much more of the past has faded in four months at Marsh View.

'Are you going to show me round?' asks Ray.

'If you'd like ... to see.'

Ray helps Arthur from his chair, lets him lean on him. 'Follow the ... yellow-brick road,' says Arthur.

They walk slowly along the yellow road, through the empty dining room and into the conservatory with its usual assortment of occupants. 'Good morning,' says Ray cheerily. 'How are you all doing? Arthur's showing me your lovely home.' He is met variously by 'good mornings', broad smiles and blank faces. 'It's great to meet you all.' And Ray takes Arthur out into the walled garden.

There is, thinks Ray, something enchanting about the garden: the cottage borders, the more ordered bedding plants, the quietness, the thin clouds drifting high overhead. 'This is so special, Arthur,' and they sit together. Ray lays his hand, quite naturally, on Arthur's and he does not object, finds it comforting. Two old friends, but one has become so much older than the other. Bustling Joan brings a tray of coffee. Matron comes across and asks Ray if he would like to stay for lunch. 'That's so good of you,' says Ray, and he will join Arthur, Yvonne and George. There is lively talk. Arthur listens contentedly but he hardly interjects. After lunch, Ray has to go. 'It's been good to see you, Arthur. I'll try not to leave it so long next time.' It has been good: Ray will keep his word and become another regular visitor to Marsh View.

'I hear you had a friend to see you today, Arthur,' says Alice when she helps him into bed. 'That must have been nice.'

Arthur looks up at her. 'Did I? ... I don't recall. ... I've had ... a sleep since then.'

Other visitors come: one-time colleagues from Spinney Hill; the Watsons; Mrs Carberry. Arthur is having fewer bad days now and is pleased to see them, although he finds it impossible to recognise them. Usually they come in pairs: they are worried about how they will find him and it makes it easier to carry on a conversation. They are surprised how much Arthur has aged since he left Rose Bank, but thankfully he has kept his sense of humour. He listens politely to their news: Spinney Hill and Thorpe have all but disappeared from his landscape, but he does not say so and he asks questions they do not understand. 'How tragic,' they say. 'An intelligent man like him, and always so fit and healthy. Mary would have hated to see him like this. But at least he seems happy enough.' It could so easily happen to any of us, they think.

And it is true, Arthur has become happier, although that may be a good or a bad thing. First it was the decline in his faculties that had made him angry. Then the diagnosis of Alzheimer's had made him angrier still and too often he had taken his anger out on Mary. His move from Rose Bank tore him away from everything he knew, and that only added to his anger. Marsh View is a caring place, but when he first arrived it had made him worse, not better. He had found himself surrounded by people who, he thought, were not like him at all. He was (and is) there to be processed: woken up, washed, dressed, fed, entertained to an extent and put to bed. Without anyone meaning it, he was being stripped of his identity, his sense of self, and he had fought against it. But the fight has been lost and there is no longer anything to be angry about. There are Alice and the garden. They are the only constants, but they are enough. They call it 'contented-demented'. 'Live for the day,' was Sarah's motto, but the exhortation has become a mockery when most days are empty and there are no more rosebuds to gather. He just takes each one as it comes, lets it envelop him. He no longer worries about his mother.

Norman does not forget what he has said and on his next visit he brings Sarah with him. Despite her age, she remains attractive and vivacious. She is wearing a boldly patterned and low-cut summer dress. Norman cannot help reflecting that her self-indulgent lifestyle, in which he has somehow become involved, has served her better than Arthur's selfless dedication to his pupils and his books. Sarah is shocked at Arthur's shrunken figure, but she does not show it and bends down to kiss him. 'Arthur, it's Sarah. How are you?'

'Sarah?'

'Sarah from Hartbourne. Do you remember?'

A half-smile crosses Arthur's face. 'Sarah? ... I wouldn't have ... you. It's been a ... long time, but I often ... think ... you.'

'I think of you, too, Arthur,' and for all sorts of reasons this is true.

'When we ... went for ... a walk. You took ... your dress ...'

'It was a long time ago, Arthur. I was a bit of a wild child.'

'And that ... evening ... Aunt Dot's ...' His twinkling eyes meet Sarah's and he holds her hand more tightly.

Norman thinks, how could I not have known? He must have been another of Sarah's conquests, the crafty devil. He sees Arthur in a different light and feels slightly cheated.

*

Sunday, 16 October. It is Arthur's seventy-eighth birthday. Flo is not going to risk taking him out so has arranged a birthday lunch at Marsh View, where there is a room that can be used for such celebrations. She has put up balloons and a 'Happy Birthday' banner and the whole family has gathered. There are all of Arthur's favourites: roast beef, cooked rare, with roast potatoes and parsnips, Yorkshire puddings and cauliflower in white sauce, followed by chocolate sponge with chocolate sauce. The cook enjoys preparing these special meals and has done them proud. Flo has brought wine (a Chateauneuf du Pape, because it is a special day) and there is a small glass of port as a treat with the coffee.

After lunch, they don coats and walk for a while in the sunlit garden; then the grandchildren, who are no longer children, play a board game that Jill has brought. Arthur loves having them with him, although he has no idea who they are. He watches, laughs, falls asleep. At tea-time, Alice and Matron come in to join them. There is a cake which Maria has made. They sing 'Happy Birthday' and ask Arthur to blow out the candle, which he manages with help from John. 'Are you going to cut the cake and make a wish, Grandad?'

Arthur takes the knife and, with John's help, cuts the first slice shakily. Who knows what he wishes, if he wishes anything at all? And who will know if his wish ever comes true? He enjoys the cake and has a second slice. Henry is obviously taken with Alice and engages her in conversation. 'Is it someone's … birthday?' asks Arthur. They are not sure if he is teasing them again.

*

Christmas is another problem for Flo and Maria. They have always had a family Christmas and it seems unthinkable to have one without Dad. However, Matron has warned against it. It can be overwhelming: too much rich food isn't good, returning to familiar surroundings can be more unsettling than after other days out, and spending nights away is especially problematic. It is not really a kindness at all. We make sure there's plenty of Christmas cheer at Marsh View – we have a little party on Christmas Eve and families are more than welcome to join in. 'Of course, it's up to you if you take Arthur out, but every year we're the ones who have to pick up the pieces.'

They confer. Although it sits unhappily, it seems better to heed Matron's advice and foregather instead at Marsh View on Christmas Eve. Jill and John put their heads together and suggest they could provide some entertainment for all the residents: they will rope in Mum and Aunt Flo, and Henry and Justin, and why not Grandad as well? Matron welcomes the idea – Sidney Smith is not around at Christmas – as long as they can come up with something everyone will enjoy. Arthur likes his music and all the grandchildren are quite musical. They decide on carol singing and Matron says it should be in the dining room, which is where they always have their party – 'We could have some safe candles on the tables, and we'll lay on Christmas food and a not too alcoholic punch. We've got plenty of extra chairs so we can squeeze in lots of visitors as well.'

They choose five carols and a Christmas poem. Jill brings her flute and John his keyboard. As darkness falls, the dining room at Marsh View is transformed into a glittering Christmas grotto and slowly it fills with the residents, their guests and the Marsh View staff. Flo introduces the family performers – Arthur is sitting with them – and they begin with 'Away in a Manger' – a children's carol, but everyone knows it. Music works its strange magic and Arthur is word-perfect, even if a little off-key. 'Silent Night', which the family sings by itself, is accompanied by Jill on her flute, its crystal notes dropping like heavenly rain. In the final verse, she plays the descant, which soars angelically above the earthbound melody.

Maria reads Thomas Hardy's poem 'The Oxen', which has always been one of her favourites. It imagines the animals worshipping the

Christ-child in the stable and balances unbelief with belief and hope:

> *So fair a fancy few would weave*
> *In these years! Yet, I feel,*
> *If someone said on Christmas Eve,*
> *'Come; see the oxen kneel,*
> *'In the lonely barton by yonder coomb*
> *Our childhood used to know,'*
> *I should go with him in the gloom,*
> *Hoping it might be so.*

As the carol singing draws to a close, the local vicar, a regular presence at Marsh View, says a prayer and gives a blessing, and there is a final, rousing rendition of 'Hark, the Herald Angels Sing'. Henry has resurrected his trumpet, last played at school, and provides a loud and brassy finale. When the applause has died down, the refreshments are taken round, and impromptu carolling breaks out here and there, and someone spills their drink, and Linda complains loudly that there's no Santa Claus and she wants to sit on his knee, and Henry is chatting to Alice, and, as he does most years, Arthur smiles benignly and declares it is his best Christmas ever.

*

It is in the cold of the New Year that Arthur takes a turn for the worse as more of the pathways in his brain become blocked or tangled. As the weeks pass, he begins to find it increasingly difficult to walk and talk, even to eat. He chooses again to spend more time in his room and more days confined to his bed. It is in February that the animals come. Sometimes they wait outside the window and sometimes they appear, unannounced, by his chair. Fortunately, he does not feel threatened by his new visitors but welcomes them as companions. They are patient. They do not judge. They understand what he says. They laugh at his jokes. Alice is disturbed when she finds Arthur talking to his new and invisible friends, but

'Hallucinations aren't unusual,' says Matron, who is quite used to such things, 'and thank goodness he doesn't see them as a threat, which does make life far more difficult. ... Don't try and persuade him they're not there – just go with the flow and talk to him about them, and pretend you can see them too. ... They'll come and go, and we needn't worry too much unless they start to upset him. ... I'll make sure everyone knows about them, and we'll have to warn Arthur's visitors in case they're taken by surprise.'

On Arthur's better days, he listens contentedly to his music and one day towards the end of April, when it is unseasonably warm, Alice takes him to his favourite spot in the walled garden, and he looks at the daffodils and the primroses, and the cherry blossom, and the clematis scrambling over the walls, and lets the scent wash over him; and he listens to the clarity of the birdsong. And in some mysterious way the garden makes connections in his brain that were broken long ago and, when Arthur closes his eyes, in that strange space between awake and asleep, fragments of the past coalesce into pictures, as in a child's kaleidoscope. He sees his mother before she was ill; Grandpa in his workshop; the playground at the village school and Mrs Jones tending to his grazed knee. There is the dormitory at Sparrowhawk Hall; the fights with the bullies of Burgoyne; and Sarah standing over him at Galleons Lap, and this time there is no shame. Now there are brighter pictures: dancing with Mary at the Graduation Ball, and lying beside her on *Still Waters*, listening to the lap-lapping of the river; the squealing of the twins as he chases them in the garden at The Moorings; Thorpe Lodge and Spinney Hill; seals at Horsey; walking the banks of the Arno; on the Rialto Bridge in Venice. There is Norman, who in recent times has proved the best of friends: had there been something between him and Mary? He remembers too many glances between them and he knows; perhaps he has always known and it was easier (or cowardly) not to confront them, and who was he to judge? But it is of no consequence now. Someone is calling, and, it seems, taking the register: 'Barnes, Belcher, Bingham, Bowler, Bowring, Bright. ... All present, Sir!' Or is it bustling Joan, always in a hurry, calling him in for lunch? 'No ... thank you. I'd rather ... stay here, if you ... don't mind.'

It is in the afternoon, when the clouds have begun to blow across, that Alice comes and sits beside him. 'Hello, Arthur, I wondered if I'd find you here. Are you feeling all right?'

He looks confused, distant, and it is hard to make out what he says. 'Quite ... all ... right.'

'It's starting to get cold. I think we'd better take you in, Arthur. How about a hot cup of tea and some cake?' With difficulty she helps him up and supports him as he shuffles inside.

'Are ... you ... Alice?' whispers Arthur.

'Yes, Arthur. Alice in wonderland.'

*

But Arthur is not all right. The doctor believes he may have had a mild stroke. He talks to Flo. 'We could move him to hospital, but apart from medication, which I can prescribe anyway, there's not much else, except tests, they can do. In fact, it might be riskier and he'll be much happier here in familiar surroundings.' Flo phones Maria, who agrees. They sense that Arthur's story is drawing to a close and, if it is, they would rather it were here.

Arthur stays in bed for a couple of days, mainly sleeping. After that he is sometimes helped to his chair, from where he can see people walking past outside, and the birds on the feeder, and the friendly robin which somehow seeks him out. He does not want to eat: a few sips of water are enough. Carers come frequently to check he is comfortable and there is a flurry of visitors whom he no longer knows. Either Flo or Maria sits with him each day.

'Promise ... you won't ... put me ... in a home,' he says.

'Promise,' says Flo. 'You're much better here.'

One evening, when Alice is drawing the curtains, the track of 'Save the Last Dance for Me' begins to play. Arthur beckons her. She can just about make out what he is saying: 'Our ... song.' He tries to stand.

'Wait a minute, Arthur. What is it you want?'

'D ... ance.'

Alice is not sure what she should do, but Arthur is agitated. 'Come on, then, Arthur. Just one dance.' He does not weigh much and she is able to lift him to his feet. He clings onto her and they begin to move slowly in time to the music. It is the least she can do for him.

A smile plays across Arthur's face. His voice is indistinct. 'Mary? ... Are you Mary?'

Alice holds him even more closely. 'Yes, Arthur. I'm Mary.' When the song ends, she leads him to his bed, washes his face and hands. 'Thank you for the dance, Arthur,' she says. It was lovely.' And she turns out the light.

In the morning, Arthur's breathing is faint and it is obvious his body is shutting down. Matron phones both Flo and Maria. They arrive as soon as they can. They talk to Arthur. He does not open his eyes and they can only hope he knows they are with him. The day passes and there is no change in his condition. Flo and Maria look through Arthur's book, share memories, laugh, stay through the night, taking it in turns to sleep. Often, either Matron or her deputy comes in to check on Arthur. The sun rises, glimpsed over the distant sea. It is another glorious day. They open the windows, breathe in the crisp and salty air. Arthur stirs. Flo calls Matron. She and Maria hold Arthur's hands, unwilling to let him go; and then it is over. As his muscles relax, he looks young again.

An early brimstone butterfly, pale yellow, flies in through the window, rests briefly on the bed, flies out again. *Mum collecting Dad,* thinks Maria She does not believe in religion and the afterlife, and is not at all superstitious, but it is with such imaginings of the spirit world that even the most sceptical are able to find solace in their grief.

*

There is a cremation, and then a remembrance service at Thorpe in St Andrew's Church: Thorpe is, after all, where Arthur is best known. More immediately, and although Matron does not like to hurry the family, his room has to be cleared. 'If you like, we can do it for you and store Arthur's things until you're ready to collect them.' She has a business to run and someone is waiting to move in. But Flo would rather do it herself and she and Dave return the following day. There are Arthur's clothes, which (if they are not too worn) will be washed and go to the charity shop; a few photographs; the watercolour of Norwich Market, which Flo would like; the painting of 'Widgeon over the Marshes' which (if Matron agrees) they would like to give to Alice; and Arthur's desk, which Maria will cherish. There are some odds and ends, and, of course, Arthur's book, and nothing else is left.

At the service, which is held one morning in July, the church is full and the sun's rays cast a golden light over the congregation. They sing 'Morning has broken', which reminds of the walled garden, and its flowers and its blackbirds. Justin reads an amusing extract from *Three Men in a Boat*, which lightens the mood, and Jill reads John Betjeman's poem 'Norfolk', about the loss of childhood innocence, although, of course, she does not know about Sarah. Norman gives the eulogy – he has known Arthur longer than anyone – but there is an etiquette about eulogies, so, like Arthur's *Story*, it is another but different work of fiction. He tells of Arthur's parents and grandparents, of exploits at Hartbourne's village school, of the challenges Arthur faced at Sparrowhawk and Burgoyne, of the university years when Arthur met Mary, of their first home aboard *Still Waters*, and of how much he will be missed as a fun-loving father and grandfather (amusing anecdotes supplied by Flo and Maria). He recalls Arthur's career as an inspirational and respected teacher at

Thorpe Lodge and Spinney Hill (more anecdotes, assiduously garnered), his success as a historian and author, his love of antiquarian books (which made him hopeless as a dealer), and the hardships of his final years. Norman also describes how Mary was the most devoted and loyal of wives, especially after Arthur's diagnosis of Alzheimer's, and he thanks the staff of Marsh View for looking after Arthur so well. 'A quiet life, a full life, and a good life. Farewell, Arthur, my old friend and God speed.' And, although no one will notice, Norman is conscious of how he has betrayed him.

Afterwards, there is a wake. The Watsons offer their condolences. Mrs Carberry says what a privilege it was to have known Arthur: 'He was always such a gentleman, in spite of his troubles.' Teachers, as old as the hills, say what a wonderful colleague he was: he always cared about his pupils, the difficult ones as much as the scholars – and he had such remarkable patience. And some of his one-time pupils have come along, too: three cheers for Sparky, to whom they owe so much. Mr Shastri beams and says how he enjoyed seeing Mr Bright every morning and how perfect it is that the sun is shining. Ray, who at his age should give up driving fast cars, hobbles around on crutches, spreading his own delicious brand of gay bonhomie. Sarah, sitting by herself, wishes that all those years ago she had written the letters she promised: would it have changed both their lives? Matron, who is accompanied by Alice, says Arthur was highly regarded at Marsh View (but such occasions are part of her job and she is practised at saying these things). Alice, who is wearing the expensive black dress she bought for her fiancé's funeral, nods in agreement but cannot bring herself to speak.

As people begin to leave, Henry says awkwardly to Alice, 'You're Alice, aren't you?'

'Yes, that's right.'

'I'm Henry, Arthur's grandson. We met at Grandad's birthday and at the Christmas party. I just wanted to thank you for looking after

Grandad so well. I know he wouldn't have survived without you. ... I thought it would be nice if we could keep in touch.'

Alice is taken aback. It is such a bizarre chat-up line, and out of place at a wake, and since the death of her fiancé she has had no desire to be chatted up. 'You can always contact me at Marsh View,' she says and turns away, embarrassed. But Henry looks so much like Arthur in the wedding photographs, and she sees in him all the gentleness, naivety and straightforwardness that Mary once saw in Arthur, and she sees he is more embarrassed than she is. On an impulse (or is it an instinct?), she picks up a napkin, writes down her mobile number and, before she leaves, hands it to Henry. 'Just in case you can't get through to Marsh View.'

It is a while before Henry summons up the courage to phone Alice, who takes more than a while before deciding to answer. His words come out in a rush: 'Alice, it's Henry, Arthur Bright's grandson. ... I hope you don't mind my calling you, but I'm coming up to Sheringham this weekend and ... wondered if you'd like to come out for a drink? ... I'll understand if you don't think it's a good idea.'

Alice, sitting alone in the walled garden after her shift has ended, hears the nervousness in his voice. In fact, she feels a bit sorry for him. But no, she thinks, it wouldn't be a good idea at all. 'Hi, Henry. That would be lovely,' she says. 'I'll really look forward to seeing you,' and she looks in surprise as a brimstone butterfly settles lightly on the soft down of her arm.

Afterword

I Am Arthur Bright: An Alzheimer's Story is a fiction – both the story and the story within the story. Arthur was never a real person, nor Mary, nor Alice, nor any of the supporting cast, but as in all literature (even fantasy literature), they have their roots in life, and many of the settings and events described in the novel are also true or partly true.

Norwich, Thorpe St Andrew, the Norfolk Broads and the North Norfolk coast are, of course, real places – although they have all changed over the years, as have the transport links, and sometimes I have slightly rearranged their geography to fit the narrative: it is what Arthur Ransome, author, journalist and spy, whose novel *Coot Club* makes a brief appearance in *I Am Arthur Bright*, called the 'romantic transfiguration of fact'.[1] However, Hartbourne, Sparrowhawk Hall, The Burgoyne School, the University of Norfolk, the King's Head, Thorpe Lodge, Warnes' boatyard, The Moorings, Mary's antique shop, Spinney Hill, Rose Bank, Mr Shastri's shop, Marsh View and the walled garden have never existed (although they, too, probably have their real-life predecessors), and Watermouth (and its University, and the dastardly Howard Kirk), invented by Malcolm Bradbury in his brilliant satirical novel *The History Man* about the 'new universities' of the 1960s, are fictions within a fiction within a fiction.

Similarly, although they have been shaped, many, but not all, of the events described in *I Am Arthur Bright* actually happened and are

---

[1] In a letter to Helen Ferris, Junior Literary Guild, US, 18 March 1937.

largely born of personal experience. Both my parents suffered from dementia, although, unlike Arthur, they were in their nineties before it became a significant problem. So Flo and Maria's eye-opening search for an acceptable residential home mirrors the search that my brother, David, and I had to make: we found the same smells of stale urine, the same homes where profit was put before patients, the lovely, civilised home that could not accept dementia residents, and even the home where the corridor was lined with brightly coloured and regularly picked paper flowers. We were fortunate that David finally discovered Cathedral View in Truro (which had no noticeable view of the cathedral), where our mother, Margaret Mary, was well cared for in her final years, if never wholly content.

Our father, Pearce Trewhella, did, embarrassingly, manage to find the wrong room in a hotel in the New Forest; sadly, he sometimes failed to recognise our mother and on occasion became aggressive towards her. He chased her in the garden, I think with a garden fork, and she had to take refuge with their friend, Pat, across the road. The tales he told became increasingly bizarre. At the age of ninety-eight, he fell at home and cut his head. There was a time when the family doctor would have stitched him up and he might have carried on, but instead he was taken to hospital where, in strange surroundings, he rapidly declined. Like Arthur Bright, he must have decided his time was up. He refused to eat, was moved to a nursing home, and died soon afterwards.

Some years later, I took our increasingly confused mother to the Memory Clinic. In *I Am Arthur Bright*, our visits are described almost verbatim. She could get lost, obsessed about her own long-dead mother, thought she was being kidnapped, took some time to settle at Cathedral View, caused a stir in the dining room, packed her suitcase to come home, tipped talcum powder over her budgerigar, and wondered how she'd found such a nice place to live. She had good days and bad days; sometimes she was delighted to see us and sometimes not. She could remember with uncanny clarity the details of her childhood but seemed not to remember sixty years of marriage. There was a rusting bird feeder outside her window. It was when she was at Cathedral View that Covid arrived and visitors were not allowed. She never caught Covid, but the restrictions were such that I suspect boredom was at least a contributory factor in her death, and I will always regret that, unlike Flo and Maria, we could not be with her in her final days.

Above all, however, *I Am Arthur Bright* is a thank-you letter to my brother, David, and his wife, Anthea. When our mother could no longer cope by herself in her sheltered flat, they took her into their own Somerset home and for two years looked after her, putting their own lives on hold. It was only when it became clear that she needed more stability and expert care that, under protest and struggling to get out of the car, she moved to Cathedral View. It was then David who put together *I Am Margaret Mary, And This Is My Story* to help keep her past alive, and that is where *I Am Arthur Bright* began.

Acknowledgements

First, my thanks to my wife, Zoë, for putting up with my writing another book: like Mary, and with some justification, she sometimes thinks we could be doing more exciting things. Secondly, thank you to those who have read and commented on early drafts of *I Am Arthur Bright*: Zoë (again), David and Anthea Lovelock, Annabel Lovelock, and, in particular, Emeritus Professor Alan Kennedy, whose wise counsel has been invaluable.

*

For those who cannot place some of the references and intertextual allusions in the novel, the following is offered as an aide memoire:

Page 2: Arthur is remembering, as much as he can, T.S. Eliot, 'The Love Song of J. Alfred Prufrock' (1915). **Page 9**: Dylan Thomas, 'Do not go gentle into that good night' (1957). **Page 13**: I recall my childhood friend, Nigel Hewitt, sending such a letter to his mother in his first week at prep school: 'Yours sincerely, Hewitt'. Not long afterwards, I read a similar letter in Anthony Buckeridge, *Jennings Goes to School* (1950). Whether Nigel had read the Jennings book, I don't know (somehow I doubt it!). **Page 24**: Galleons Lap is the magical place at the end of A.A. Milne, *The House at Pooh Corner* (1928), where Christopher Robin says goodbye to Pooh and his childhood. **Page 28**: Grandpa is referring to Laurie Lee's, *Cider with Rosie* (1959), chapter 12, in which Lee recounts his first sexual encounter. **Page 63**: The University of Watermouth is the creation of Malcolm Bradbury in *The History Man* (1975). Howard Kirk is the 'history man' himself, a trendy sociology lecturer and serial seducer of both colleagues and students. **Page 65**: Leonard Cohen, 'Suzanne', published as a poem in 1966 and performed by Cohen in 1967 on the album *Songs of Leonard Cohen*. **Page 71**: 'Gather ye rosebuds while ye may' – the first line of Robert Herrick's poem, 'To the Virgins, to Make Much of Time' (1648). Also on p. 177. **Page 72**: 'Ill met by moonlight.' From William Shakespeare, *A Midsummer Night's Dream* (1595-6), Act II, scene 1. **Page 100**: Miss Scarlett is a character in *Cluedo*, a detective board game in which participants compete to identify the name of the murderer, the place of the crime, and the weapon used. **Page 129**: In Arthur Ransome, *Coot Club* (1934), 'Hullaballoos' was the name for noisy and destructive holidaymakers on the Norfolk Broads. **Page 169**: 'Oh I do like to be beside the seaside' (1907) – a popular music hall song by John H. Glover. 'We'll Meet Again' (1939), a wartime song, by Ross Parker and Hughie Charles, made famous by Vera Lynn, the 'forces sweetheart'. **Page 186**: 'Save the Last Dance for Me' (1960) – song by Doc Pomus and Mort Shuman. **Page 187**: Jerome K. Jerome, *Three Men in a Boat* (1889); John Betjeman, 'Norfolk' (1954), which laments the loss of childhood innocence.

By the Same Author

Swallows, Amazons and Coots: A Reading of Arthur Ransome
From Morality to Mayhem: the Fall and Rise of the English School Story
The Business of Reading: A Hundred Years of the English Novel
Where All the Ladders Start: A Study of Poems, Poets and the People who Inspired Them

---

Cover illustration:
Citroenvlinder (Brimstone Butterfly). Photograph (2014) by Rene Mensen.
Licenced under Creative Commons Attribution Generic 2.0.